Ans	05/09 AR	M.L.	
ASH	9/01	MLW	
Bev		Mt.Pl	
C.C.		NLM	Kale 4/07
C.P.		Ott	
Dick		PC	
DRZ		PH	
ECH		P.P.	
ECS		Pion.P.	
Gar	10/08	Q.A.	
GRM		Riv	
GSP		RPP	
G.V.		Ross	
Har		S.C.	
JPCP		St.A.	
KEN		St.J	
K.L.		St.Joa	
K.M.	8/09	St.M.	
L.H.		Sgt	
LO		T.H.	4/08
Lyn		TLLO	
L.V.		T.M.	
McC		T.T.	
McG		Ven	
McQ		Vets	
MIL		VP	
		Wat	
		Wed	
		WIL	1/08 (Joost)
		W.L.	

BURY BY NIGHT

As the seaside village of Gifford basks in the June sun, the peace is shattered when the body of Simon Connolly is discovered, buried in another person's grave. Who struck him down, and what has become of his fiancée, Lily Sullivan? Detective Inspector Moss Coen arrives from Dublin, with his assistant, to investigate. When two people die suddenly and violently, Geraldine Lovell — Connolly's former fiancée — becomes involved . . . The solution eventually becomes clear — but not before the Inspector's assistant, Finnbarr Raftery, comes close to a watery end.

Books by Lorette Foley
in the Linford Mystery Library:

MURDER IN BURGOS

LORETTE FOLEY

BURY
BY
NIGHT

Complete and Unabridged

LINFORD
Leicester

First published in Great Britain
by Robert Hale Limited
London

First Linford Edition
published 2007
by arrangement with
Robert Hale Limited
London

British Library CIP Data

Foley, Lorette
 Bury by night.—Large print ed.—
Linford mystery library
 1. Murder—Investigation—Ireland—Fiction
 2. Police—Ireland—Fiction 3. Detective and
 mystery stories 4. Large type books
 I. Title
 823.9'14 [F]

 ISBN 978–1–84617–677–7

Published by
F. A. Thorpe (Publishing)
Anstey, Leicestershire

Set by Words & Graphics Ltd.
Anstey, Leicestershire
Printed and bound in Great Britain by
T. J. International Ltd., Padstow, Cornwall

1

Detective Inspector Maurice Coen sat at a desk in his none too tidy office and looked out of the window at the Castle Yard beneath. The morning sunlight gave it a pleasant air and soothed him as he smoked. On his knees reposed a file newly typed up and indexed; the case history of a two to three months old (so far unidentified) body, male, found at Gifford where an inquest was being held that day.

Brooding on the meagre details, he knew he had seen too many small towns shut their doors to a police investigation, and for this probably eventually fruitless job he had been given a new assistant — new in every sense. From under the desk blotter he withdrew a sheet of official headed paper and read the notification once again. He turned to the window and went on smoking.

It would be hard to guess which

thoughts remained uppermost in his mind when he glanced across to the subject of the document, a tall, very tall, fair-haired and slightly rawboned young man with exceptionally large feet and hands, who obscured rather than occupied the chair on which he sat and made pretty Miss Curran, posting to and from the filing cabinet, seem like a delicate fairy.

The thing was to know how to begin, he said to himself. Once the job was in hand, routine would take over and he could be detached, impersonal. Next time . . . but he hoped there would not be a next time. He ran short stubby fingers through his stiff straight dark hair.

'Detective Raftery!' he said suddenly.

The young man got up off the chair in one continuous movement. 'Sir,' he said.

The Inspector waved him down with an impatient hand.

'I dare say they taught you a load of stuff during your training. A lot of it you'll have to forget if you work with me. For a start, I can't stand regimentation, or other claptrap. I'm Moss and this is Sheila.'

Miss Curran flushed slightly and said: 'Hello.'

Detective Raftery smiled briefly and contemplated his feet. When he looked up it was to find Moss staring at him.

He hesitated, then said: 'My name's Finnbarr — Finny if you like.'

'Finny,' repeated Miss Curran, smiling at him.

'How old are you?' asked Moss.

'Twenty-three.'

Moss frowned suddenly, and with a movement of his hand seemed to sweep away the frown. He collected various papers and stuffed them into an already bulging briefcase.

'Better get going. An hour's drive to Gifford. No use in telling you about the case. You'll hear it all at the inquest. All there is to know,' he added gloomily.

His departure from the room left a clean swept desk and efficient Miss Curran still briskly filing. Out in the Castle Yard, he said: 'My car is parked over by the gates; the dark green four-door. Here's the keys.'

He got into the passenger seat and sat

back, not appearing to notice Finny's expert manoeuvrings. The car turned into Dame Street and headed for College Green.

'I suppose you've driven your father quite a bit,' Moss said casually, 'or did he always drive himself to the Courts?'

'I used to drive him sometimes,' Finny said more easily. 'He's getting on a bit now.'

'Enjoying his retirement?'

'No.' For the first time Finny laughed. 'I think he's a bit at a loose end. He has his golf of course, but he needs to keep his mind active. He reads a great deal.'

Moss's thick eyebrows shot up and his vivid blue eyes opened just for a second.

'Yes,' he said. 'Judge Raftery weighed his verdicts with care, so he did.' He was aware of the edge to his voice, and Finny, hearing it, was silent.

Gifford, a seaboard town as the inhabitants like to call it, in reality a mushrooming village, is thirty miles or so from Dublin city, depending upon whether you take the coast or inland roads. The resident population numbers

4

about four hundred persons but during the summer months this total more than doubles, as Gifford with its sandy beaches, three hotels, various guest-houses and houses-to-let, opens its doors (in the literal sense only) to the holidaymaker, its principal source of income.

Apart from its small shops, the town's industries are those of agriculture (mainly crops) and fisheries, for Gifford has a good if small harbour which in addition to the deep-sea trawlers also houses the local yacht club.

The police station is in Market Square opposite the Market Cross Hotel and here Inspector Coen and Detective Raftery duly arrived and were greeted by Sergeant Tom O'Shea.

'We had a telephone call to be expecting ye, Inspector, and none too soon to my way of thinking, for there's been an important development.'

Sergeant O'Shea, a tall hawk-faced Kerryman, with parched and lined cheeks and a hooked and dominant nose, so closely resembled an American Indian as to be incongruous in the navy blue uniform of the Garda Siochana. His speech was indeed English but his accent such that visitors from that country were apt to believe it to be Gaelic.

Moss shook hands in a perfunctory way, commandeered a desk, opened his briefcase and proceeded to spread out the contents. The Sergeant was not offended but on the contrary very impressed.

'They've sent us a good man, he's that quick; aye, knows what he's about and no nonsense. It's going to be big, woman, they'd not have sent his like for a small affair.' All this was confided to Mrs. O'Shea at a late hour. For the present, the Sergeant was imparting details of what had just occurred.

'We had an identification of the body an hour ago. Garda Noonan here had to hold the woman up, the poor dear. Aye, terrible it was. But she's sure, yes, quite sure that it's her son, Simon Connolly. He was aged nineteen and they thought he was away to England, and never suspected harm come to him.'

'How is she that sure?' enquired Moss

cautiously, with visions of a live Simon returning home in the midst of his investigations.

'Well do ye see, the body's not what ye'd call decomposed, for all it's not such a pleasant sight, as ye'll see for yourself. And then he had a broken front tooth crowned four or five years ago, at the Dental Hospital she said. We'll be able to check that anyway, but it's gold d'ye see and it's not likely she'd be mistaken.'

'Well I suppose we will have the whole thing laid bare at the inquest,' said Moss, relieved, 'or is it going to be that kind of affair?'

Sergeant O'Shea was surprised and flattered by this deference which, had he but known it, arose from disinterest on the part of the investigating officer. Throughout the interview, Detective Raftery maintained a discreet silence and did his best to absorb the information proffered, in the unlikely event of his being called upon to give an opinion.

Later, seated at a very nice table by the window of the Market Cross Hotel dining-room (of course everyone in the hotel knew who they were) Moss said conversationally: 'Ever attended an inquest before?'

'Er . . . two, no three in fact,' replied Finny nervously. This fellow was going to be difficult to work for. He invited informality; he wouldn't let you stay at a respectful distance. Then when you got in close, he'd chop you up. He'd have to be careful, but looking at Moss's short restless fingers making imaginary patterns around the salt and peppers, he doubted his own ability.

'Accident cases?' went on Moss a little absently.

'Two were, yes. Drownings. An elderly man and a sixteen-year-old boy. The last was a hit and run; a little girl, two years old.' Finny coughed.

'Well that's some experience anyway.' Moss relapsed into silence, but his fingers continued to make patterns on the damask cloth.

Altogether, Finny was glad to be back at the station again, where they collected the Sergeant. All three men made their way to the Vocational School in the gymnasium of which the inquest was being held. The centre of the oblong-shaped room had been cleared of its normal equipment and seats borrowed from various classrooms had been set out in rows. To one side and with their backs to the rows of parallel bars would sit the jury, while on the other side were some seats for the Inspector and his colleagues.

The Coroner arrived and was introduced; a short spare man with gold-rimmed spectacles and a great precision of speech. His name was Walsh.

The room was already full, and on the seats reserved for the witnesses, Moss saw a woman of forty-odd dressed in black and with a young lad of about fifteen at her side. Next was a rather striking-looking girl with long straight red hair and a creamy complexion and beyond her a well-dressed man and woman who might have been brother and sister but who were, said Sergeant O'Shea in response to Moss's whispered enquiry, the doctor and a local schoolteacher. After that came a little chip of a man, no taller than five feet, his skin dry with age but agile yet on his feet, giving the appearance of a modern leprechaun.

The jury members were brought in and duly sworn, and the first witness was called to give evidence of finding the body. This witness proved to be the leprechaun man.

'You are Jack Finnegan, a retired cemetery official,' the Coroner began, looking at his notes and apparently not wishing to give offence by asking that question.

'I am indeed and eighty-two year old last November,' said the leprechaun man proudly.

Mr. Walsh smiled thinly. 'Quite so, Mr. Finnegan, quite so. Would you be kind enough now to describe the events which led to the discovery of the body?'

'It was the Casey funeral last week,' said Mr. Finnegan, taking out an evil-looking pipe and lighting it with some difficulty.

Finny, appalled, looked for signs of wrath from the official party and a stern condemnation from Mr. Walsh, but Mr. Walsh merely poured himself a glass of water and slightly shielded his face while the offender, between puffs, continued with his long and circumlocutory story.

'Old Mrs. Casey would have been ninety-five next August. A grand old woman, strong you know. Of course she wasn't a Casey by birth — she was born Emma Duffy.' The old man paused, and Mr. Walsh got in a question:

'She was buried in the Duffy grave, was she?'

'Oh no, that grave was closed many the year ago, that and the one next to it. Two branches of the Duffy family and they had graves side by side. That grave was closed,' Mr. Finnegan paused and waved his pipe aloft, 'that grave was closed when old Mrs. Casey's father died,' he screwed up his little wizen face in an effort of concentration, 'and he died in 1926.'

A titter went round the room and the Coroner shook his head warningly.

'Was she buried in the Casey grave then?'

'We may all be dead and buried before we come to the end of this,' Moss grumbled under his breath.

11

'She was,' continued Mr. Finnegan. 'That grave was first opened in 1902 when her husband Jim's father was buried in it, and it is the last grave but one to the boundary wall.'

'And what grave is next to the boundary wall?' Mr. Walsh asked mildly.

'Why, the grave the deceased was found in; Martha Payne and her husband's grave — he was Jim too.'

'And how did you come to find the deceased's body?' pursued Mr. Walsh.

Thereupon Mr. Finnegan began a long rambling discourse on how he had arisen at 7 a.m. (his usual time of rising) had thought he would just drop down the road to his late place of employment, which indeed he often visited, on account of its being the day of Mrs. Casey's funeral. He felt there might still have been some work to do on the grave itself, but had found everything in readiness, neat mounds of clay piled on either side.

A gratified cough came from a member of the audience and Mr. Finnegan, whose hearing appeared to be remarkable for his age, looked around and identified the person.

'Aye, Kevin Bates,' he said, 'I known good work when I seen it. ''Course,' he added confidentially to Mr. Walsh, 'it was I had the training of him.'

Moss crossed and uncrossed his legs, worked up his hair and then smoothed it down, but the Coroner persisted in the same unruffled manner.

'And did you notice anything unusual, Mr. Finnegan?'

'I saw Martha Payne's grave had sunk.'

'And why was that unusual?'

'Well, it would be ten years and more since she died.' The little man began an explanation, but Mr. Walsh skilfully headed him off by saying that of course he was the expert in these matters and while Mr. Finnegan absorbed this compliment Mr. Walsh got in another question.

'What did you do then?'

'I looked at it and looked, and couldn't make no sense of it, and then I went to Kevin Bates here, at his house, and told him and he said he hadn't noticed. So then we both came back and he was as puzzled as myself. We said we'd level the surface a bit and of course when we put our shovels in we knew something was up, for the clay wasn't hard at all. So I said to him, let's dig down a way, and we did and Kevin was for stopping then, but I says there's only two people in that grave and no harm to go down a bit further, so we went on and then we found the blanket.'

The audience whose attention had wandered during Mr. Finnegan's recital, stirred at the last word.

'You found a blanket?' prompted the Coroner.

'Aye, and it gave me a bit of a turn and I said to Kevin here to go careful then, not knowing what we might find, and sure enough we found more of the blanket at the other end of the grave, so I says to Kevin to get a trowel and scrape away the clay at the top, and that's how we found him, the poor fellow,' concluded Mr. Finnegan.

'Perhaps you would kindly describe to us the condition in which you found the body?'

Mr. Finnegan paused and looked doubtful. 'It was a bit disagreeable,' he began, but the Coroner interrupted:

'I merely wished you to say if the body were clothed.'

'Oh yes,' said Mr. Finnegan, relieved. 'Yes, he had a full suit of clothes on, and a shirt and tie as well.'

'And did you recognise the man?'

Mr. Finnegan turned round and regarded the lady in black.

'I understand . . . ' he began.

The Coroner stopped him. 'Did you yourself recognise this man?'

'No,' said Jack Finnegan, regretfully Finny thought.

Mr. Finnegan was succeeded by Mr. Bates who corroborated all of the foregoing, merely adding in answer to a question from the Coroner that upon discovery of the body, he had cycled into the village to inform the local Gardai. After Mr. Bates, came Sergeant O'Shea whose evidence was of a formal nature. In reply to the Coroner's question about identification, he said: no, he had not been able to identify the deceased.

That disposed of the Sergeant and the next witness called was Dr. O'Brien. The jury sat up expectantly and the audience became tense. In answer to some preliminary questions, the doctor stated that he was Dr. John O'Brien attached to the local hospital and that he had carried out a post-mortem on the deceased who was a well-nourished adult male in his late teens or early twenties. In his opinion death had occurred at least two months previously or, dependent upon weather and other conditions, possibly twice that period.

After describing in some detail the condition in which he found the body, the samples of the various organs which he had removed and which had been sent to the State Pathologist's Office, he went on to describe the injuries the deceased had sustained.

'In your view,' said Mr. Walsh carefully, 'were these injuries sufficient to cause death?'

The doctor looked surprised. 'Certainly they were the cause of death,' he said. 'The base of the skull was crushed; death must have been immediate.'

'Is it possible he might have met with an accident?'

'It is barely possible,' replied the doctor composedly, 'but only if he had had a severe fall. However, in that case I should expect to see other serious damage. Or, if a heavy object had fallen on him, he would need to be in a stooping position when it hit him, and there should then be subsequent injury to the face at least, and of which I found none.'

The Coroner nodded approvingly. Mr. Walsh then removed his gold-rimmed spectacles, polished them with his snow-white handkerchief and replaced them briskly on his nose.

'Now,' he said, with an air of gathering everything together into one question, 'having regard to the nature of the injuries, their extent and position, please tell us how you believe death to have been caused.'

The doctor seemed to take a deep breath. 'I believe he was hit from behind, with a large and jagged implement, possibly a stone, and that death was practically instantaneous.'

'I see,' said the Coroner. 'Could the deceased's head have been forcibly knocked against an object such as you describe, on the ground — a rock for example?'

'Certainly,' said the doctor, 'however in that case, as in the others I mentioned, there would be further signs of violence, on the shoulders, for example.'

'And you did not find any such signs?'

'I did not.'

The all-male jury at this point looked like so many large rabbits with ears cocked.

Mr. Walsh consulted his watch. 'I will now order a short adjournment,' he said concisely, 'to enable the jury to view the body, and afterwards,' he went on graciously, with an eye to the pathetic figure of Mrs. Connolly, 'we will have the formal evidence of identification.'

Mrs. Connolly raised her head for a moment and her son reached forward and clasped her hands.

Rather a nice gesture for a fifteen-year-old and in public too, thought Finny as the jury shuffled out. He wondered how they stood it. What if he, Finny Raftery, were dead and his mother and brother

Charlie sat there. Supposing it had happened to them? And in thinking along these lines, he came close to anticipating later events.

During the interval, Moss and Sergeant O'Shea were deep in subdued conversation. Finny caught a murmured reference to the Kerry football team. For once Moss was actually smiling.

Then the jury returned, looking very quiet, and the hearing resumed immediately with the evidence of Mrs. Connolly who gave her name as Margaret Connolly, widow, of Moy Farm, Gifford, the mother of two sons and two daughters, all unmarried. Mr. Walsh questioned her very kindly, albeit with a certain briskness.

'Now,' he said, 'you have told us of your two sons, Simon the elder, and Brendan who is present here today,' he nodded towards the young boy seated. 'You have seen the body of the deceased and have heard the evidence given of the finding of the body and the probable cause of death. Do you positively identify the body as that of your son, Simon Connolly?'

'I do,' she said simply.

'Without any doubt at all?'

'Yes.'

Finny now expected to hear again about the broken front tooth, but the Coroner passed on to another matter.

'Your son Simon lived at home with you?'

'Yes, until last February.'

'What happened in February?'

'He went away to England, and got a job there.'

'Do you know that he actually arrived there?'

'Well,' Mrs. Connolly paused slightly, 'we had a letter from him saying he had found work and was living in digs.'

'Was this the only communication from your son?'

'He didn't write again,' she said. Mrs. Connolly seemed to falter for a moment, and Finny thought she was going to give way suddenly, but in the end she took out a handkerchief, wiped her eyes and blew her nose, and went on more steadily. 'I have the letter here,' she said. 'I brought it in case it should be wanted.'

Mr. Walsh brightened. 'That was very good of you,' he said. 'May I read it?'

She handed it to him and having read it aloud he passed it to the jury for their inspection. Headed with a Manchester address and beginning 'Dear Ma', it said the writer had been fixed up with a job and Lily was working in an office and was pleased. Everything was fine and they were not to worry if he didn't write for a while. It was dated March 3rd and signed 'Simon'.

'Now,' said Mr. Walsh, adding to his notes and pausing while he did so, 'yes, now this letter refers to a 'Lily' getting a job in an office. Do you know who Lily is?'

'Lily Sullivan.'

'A friend of your son's?'

'They had just got engaged.' Suddenly Mrs. Connolly looked across to the girl with the red hair and burst out: 'Oh my dear, I'm so sorry.'

'Don't fret,' replied the girl.

The Coroner looked at her with some slight deference and tapped his fingers softly on his notes.

'We will come to that in a moment,' he said, 'now, Mrs. Connolly do you know where Lily Sullivan is at present?'

'She hasn't written, and I don't know where she is.'

'And don't care either from the sound of it,' added Moss in a low voice.

'Who is the girl they spoke to?' Finny whispered across to Sergeant O'Shea.

The Sergeant grinned. 'That's Miss Geraldine Lovell — only daughter of the local big-shot.'

Meanwhile the Coroner was asking about Miss Sullivan's home address.

'I believe she came from Limerick, but I didn't know the address. She used to work at the post office here, so perhaps Miss Purcell . . . '

'Miss Purcell being the sub-postmistress, of course,' interposed the Coroner swiftly. 'Yes, that should present no difficulty. Mrs. Connolly,' he went on, 'your son went to England in February of this year and appeared to write to you from there in March, just three months ago. Can you tell us of any reason why his body should be found here, buried?'

'I cannot,' she cried out, 'who would kill him? He never harmed anyone. He was always a quiet decent boy and he was never in trouble.'

Moss smiled grimly. 'They never are,' he muttered.

The next witness proved to be the tall red-haired girl, who stated in a composed way that she was Geraldine Lovell of Furry Park House, Gifford, and a former fiancée of the deceased.

Detective Raftery moved forward rather sharply, but the only other persons who evinced any signs of surprise were a number of newspaper reporters at the back of the room. The Coroner, who had been polite to each of the witnesses in turn, continued his smooth progress with Miss Lovell.

'You have said that you were previously engaged to Simon Connolly. When was that please?'

'From July of last year until the beginning of this February.'

'I see. And in consequence of what happening was the engagement broken off in February?'

'He'll be lucky if he gets a straight answer to that one,' whispered Sergeant O'Shea, but Miss Lovell appeared to have no such inhibitions.

'Simon told me he wanted to marry Lily instead,' she replied coolly.

'The press boys must be enjoying this lot,' Moss glanced over his shoulder to where three gentlemen of the press were busy scribbling and, even as he spoke, one of them got up and left the room. 'Just make the final evening edition,' remarked the Inspector *sotto voce*.

In reply to a further question from Mr. Walsh, the witness said she had accompanied Mrs. Connolly to see the body, in response to Mrs. Connolly's appeal to her to do so.

'I am sure we all sympathise with you in what must have been a most distasteful task for a young girl,' said the Coroner in his prim way. 'However, I must ask you if you entirely agree with Mrs. Connolly that the body is that of your late fiancé and her son, Simon Connolly?'

'There is no doubt of any kind in my mind.'

The Coroner smiled well satisfied, and Finny, who some years previously, had taken part in several school musical productions, notably *The Gondoliers* was now tempted to break into a chorus of: 'Of that there is no manner of doubt, no probable possible shadow of doubt, no possible doubt whatever.' Indeed, he was beginning to feel that if he did not sing or have a drink or go for a long walk, his head would burst.

Miss Lovell was followed by the lady whom Sergeant O'Shea had pointed out as a local schoolteacher. She gave her name as Miss Rachel Payne, and her evidence had been requested as the owner of the grave in which the body had been discovered.

She had a trim well-controlled figure, costumed in check tweed of a grey-green character, and topped with a pale blue silk blouse fastened at the neck by a pearl brooch. On her softly waved grey hair, she wore a closely fitting navy hat with a small brim turned down at the front. The precision of her speech almost rivalling that of Mr. Walsh, she contrived in a few sentences to convey shock that her late parents' grave should be so desecrated.

Mr. Walsh asked if she had known the deceased and she softened slightly and said: yes, many years ago he had been a pupil at St. Rose of Lima's girls school where they also took in boys of under eight years of age. During his last year at that school, she had been his teacher.

With considerable temerity, everyone felt, Mr. Walsh then enquired if she knew of any reason at all why the body of Simon Connolly should have been placed in a grave belonging to her family, but she replied quite simply that she knew of no reason.

No other witnesses were called, the Coroner summed up concisely the evidence presented, and the jury after only a few minutes deliberation gave a verdict of 'murder by a person or persons unknown,' a verdict which Finny Raftery confidently expected but which Inspector Coen would have been reluctant to predict.

2

The following morning Moss surveyed his forces gathered in the back room of the police station, converted into an office for the duration. Miss Curran, urgently summoned from Dublin together with some necessary office equipment; she and it would be arriving shortly in a police van. This had been accomplished with the minimum of fuss, as the Sergeant so remarked to Moss.

'The last upset we had here, not counting Miss Payne's brooch being lost, and that was recovered — the last big affair we had an inspector down here for, mentioning no names mind, he was awful for the red tape. Nothing but was done in triplicate.'

'Was it murder?' asked Moss.

'Sure that we never knew. There wasn't a bit of proof to be got anywhere. The locals knew, it's my belief, but they kept it close. Aye, close is the word.'

Moss sighed: 'That's the way in these country places. They won't betray their own, whatever they've done. At the inquest yesterday, the witnesses were very frank. Does that mean they're as much in the dark as we are?'

The Sergeant hesitated. 'Perhaps,' he said.

This conversation was in Moss's mind when he addressed himself to marshalling his rather meagre forces.

'We won't have the clothes or the blanket back from the forensic boys until tomorrow, so we'll have to begin without them, and the first thing I want to get settled is when Simon Connolly arrived back in this country, who saw him and when, and, most important, where is Lily Sullivan now?'

'You don't think something could have happened to her?' said Finny sharply.

'Another body in another grave? What do you think, Tom?'

'No, no, surely it could not be that,' the Sergeant was genuinely shocked.

'Oh, we shall probably find her safe enough in Manchester, or wherever she may have moved to by now. The thing is, from the evidence at the inquest, only one person had a real motive and that motive pushed far enough might have removed Lily Sullivan.'

'Miss Lovell,' exclaimed the Sergeant in an awed voice, while Finny stared in amazement.

Moss regarded their disbelieving faces. 'She said quite openly that he jilted her for this Lily person — I wonder why by the way — unless of course Lily was something very special, but then Miss Lovell has looks and money; an almost irresistible combination.'

'She's a young thing and cannot leave her mother,' said Finny for no reason he was aware of. The other two looked at him and, conscious of their scrutiny, he got up suddenly and went over to the window.

'She's Martin Lovell's only child,' said the Sergeant, and there was a warning note in his voice.

'And the bold Martin is a man to be reckoned with, eh? I admit it's hardly likely hers could be the hand that did the deed or buried him afterwards, but that's not to say she couldn't have an accomplice, a lover perhaps — anyone around here fit that picture?'

'I'd say she's had a good number of lads around her since she was fourteen, but I'd not heard of any special fellow till she engaged herself to young Connolly.'

'Could have been one though,' said Moss. 'Even in a place like this, I bet some things get kept quiet.'

'Not with Miss Purcell at the post office,' said O'Shea with a grin.

'What's Miss P. like?'

'Lived here all her life; knows everyone's business as well as her own.'

'In other words, could tell us a mouthful?'

'Aye, if she chose to, but if it's one of her own people, I mean the ones who've lived here always, she'll tell ye nothing.'

'We'll apply to her first about Lily Sullivan anyway. The girl may have written to her. In fact if Lily is in the land of the living, you'd think she'd write to someone about her intended being missing for three months at a go, and no word.'

'Aye,' said the Sergeant, with a dawning respect. 'I hadn't looked at it that way. It's queer right enough. We'll not be able to do much today anyhow,' he added, 'they'll all be away to the funeral.'

'Well,' countered Moss, 'it'll be only decent to put in an appearance ourselves and we may spot something of interest.'

Finny, still at the window, saw the emergence of Sheila Curran from a small navy blue van. She stepped briskly onto the path and made her way through the low gate which stood open. Presently she was directed into the inner room.

'We've a problem on our hands here, Sheila,' was Moss's greeting.

'I see you have,' said Miss Curran.

Moss grinned. 'Been reading the morning papers, eh?'

'None of them compare with last night's *Evening Reporter*. It has a huge picture of Geraldine Lovell leaving the inquest with Mrs. Connolly and all the details of the broken engagement.'

'How did we miss that?' said Moss in

mock consternation.

'Final edition, most likely,' replied the Sergeant.

'I saved a copy for you.' Miss Curran opened her travelling case and took out a folded newspaper which she gave to Moss.

He read it through briefly, still grinning. At the end, he broke into a laugh and pushed the paper into the Sergeant's outstretched hand.

The police party arrived at the cemetery well before the cortège and, Moss having parked the car, they began a reconnaissance of the terrain. The burial ground was situated at the end of a winding lane which swelled out into a horseshoe at its terminus, slightly to one side of the main gateway.

Inside the gate, a gravelled path led past old and grassy mounds covering the dead of two centuries and past two gigantic chestnut trees, landmarks in that flat country. A hot sun beat down upon Moss and Finny walking along. The birds in the chestnut trees chirruped and sang, and in the tall dry grass of long-neglected graves, the grasshoppers creaked.

The diminutive figure of Mr. Finnegan could be seen hurrying along the path towards them, his slightly bowed legs giving him a rolling gait. He greeted the Inspector as an old friend though he had not previously spoken to him and, without preamble, launched into his usual discursive speech.

'It's at the far end here, y'see where the wall comes round, circular like. Very sheltered at the other side of the wall, with the trees of Lisk Farm there at the back.'

Moss looked in the direction of Jack's pointing finger and saw an irregular line of trees just visible above the high wall.

'How high is the wall there?' he asked.

'Ten foot, maybe eleven. Whoever would have put him over, he'd have had a hard job.'

'It looks as if whoever it was handled the body very carefully, from the evidence of the doctor. What do you think?' asked Moss.

Mr. Finnegan nodded emphatically. 'Sure they did, and the blanket they put him in was sewn up too at the sides.'

Moss's eyebrows shot up, and Mr. Finnegan looked at him delightedly. 'Thought they would have mentioned it at the inquest,' the old man said, 'but they never did. In too much of a hurry, very like.'

They had reached the boundary wall now and he turned left to follow the path which ran seven or eight feet inside it. Here the headstones backed onto the wall, and very shortly they came to that inscribed to the memory of James Payne and his wife. Moss looked at it for a moment and then turned round to inspect the Casey grave on the opposite side of the path, where a moderate sized but doughty angel hovered over a granite slab commemorating Patrick and his son, James.

A warning bell sounded away in the distance and Mr. Bates came on the scene to attend to his official duties. The Inspector viewed the arrival of the mourners. Mrs. Connolly and her son Brendan, he readily identified, and the two young girls with them he supposed were the daughters, Dorothy and Anne. Supporting Mrs. Connolly on her left arm was a lean well-built man of thirty or so.

Behind this front party came an assorted band of relatives and friends in sombre hues. After a short ceremony, in which the officiating priest recited the prayers and blessed the coffin, the body of Simon Connolly returned to the ground from which it had been uncovered the week before. Mr. Bates's assistant then rattled a wide board across the gaping hole and proceeded to cover this with the numerous floral tributes. After which the immediate relatives departed, while the remainder of the attendance stood around uneasily, before they too began to drift away, walking slowly down the path towards the gate.

Moss allowed the last of them to move off before he followed, and on reaching the exit he found the mourners re-assembled and rather more animated. A stationwagon had been pulled up near the gate and here a jovial and prosperous-looking man was dispensing small glasses of whisky.

Few of those present had apparently refused, noted Moss, edging his way towards the back of the group.

A further half-hour passed, during which the detective found himself in conversation with a short bald man who turned out to be a first cousin of the late Peter Connolly, father of Simon. His name was Turlough McClintock, said this man, and he was a farmer from County Westmeath. Very soon, Moss knew of the exact location of Mr. McClintock's one hundred acre farm, portion of which had caused its owner anxiety in the past, as it was bog land, but now with the price of fuels Mr. McClintock's bog was more than paying its way; in fact he had recently acquired a machine cutter. From the subject of turf, the farmer passed easily to the topic of sheep, fifty or sixty of which he had grazing on his other piece of poor land, which was hilly. Mr. McClintock's woolly sheep were mentally rounded up for Moss's approval, he being told of their handling and care and the price now obtainable for wool which at one time his father had not even bothered to sell.

Moss headed off a lecture on the subject of Mr. McClintock's thirty dairy cows by saying he wondered how the farmer could afford time away from so many demanding activities, and the man agreed seriously but said that for the sake of his friendship with the boy's dead father he just had to come.

Moss said these sentiments did Mr. McClintock credit and Mr. McClintock said Moss was a good fellow and shook his hand warmly and invited him to call at the McClintock farm if ever he should be in its neighbourhood. He said he would not trouble the widow or her family just now (which news Moss felt must have brought them relief had they but heard it). However, if they should need help or advice they knew where to find him and he would come at once no matter what the difficulty.

The Inspector was beginning to wonder if he should ever be able to free himself from the web of the other's conversation, when all at once he espied Miss Payne moving through the crowd and making as if to depart. With a hasty word to his companion, Moss moved forward to intercept her. As he reached the schoolteacher and endeavoured with a sign to draw her to one side, he found Turlough McClintock still at his heels.

'Rachel,' said that man triumphantly, 'funerals do bring together those connected, eh?'

Miss Payne flushed up under her severe black hat.

'Why, Terry,' she said rather timidly, 'how nice to see you again after all this time.'

He pumped her hand (Moss was forcefully reminded of the thirty dairy cows) and enquired after her sister in New Zealand.

'Clara is very well, thank you,' her sister responded politely. 'She and Don are still living near Auckland.'

'And how is the family; your nieces must be grown-up now?'

'Yes, the three girls. The eldest will be getting married shortly, and I have never seen any of them. They are very kind, inviting me to stay with them for a holiday or to sell up here and go out to live with them, and I should like to go, except . . . ' Miss Payne paused awkwardly, and then went on with a rush, 'of course while dear Mama was alive I couldn't go, and you see now there is the school — I should miss that terribly.'

Moss retreated. There was work to be done at the grave.

Afterwards, Finny looked back to the beginnings of the case and the curious contentment of that sunny afternoon. The wall, to the top of which he with difficulty hoisted himself, was certainly uncomfortable, its stones being granite and irregular. Immediately below him, the squat bulk of Moss's figure moved about, the deft fingers probing carefully. His own were less sure and certainly slower, but at the end of an hour they had between them a collection of assorted items. No marks had been found consistent with the dragging of a body over the top of the wall at that particular point, and a search of the ground outside the walls revealed a dog food tin, a sardine tin, two cigarette butts, a hair clip, an empty cigarette packet and an envelope addressed to a Miss Rita Mulholland at a Dublin address.

From the top of the wall and the wall itself, Finny had collected several strands of human hair, another cigarette butt, a sweet paper and the inevitable leaves, weeds and bits of moss. The other Moss had meanwhile finished his inspection of the grave surrounds. Two match sticks, a broken shovel, and a jamjar had been found, and he was now sifting the surface clay, dug up yet again by the obliging Mr. Bates. This tiresome job produced quite a pile of stones, a grey button and a small gold earring suitable for pierced ears.

Finny at length ventured to say (somewhat incoherently, for he was out of breath): 'Do you not think we could do with extra manpower on this case — official I mean?'

Moss straightened up, holding his back.

A shout from Kevin interrupted whatever he was going to say, and he leant forward to view the article which Mr. Bates with difficulty detached from its position deep in the ground, and flush with the headstone. An object which, as Jack Finnegan said in his picturesque way, 'put the heart across all of them.'

It was a square brass plate and it was engraved:

Simon Anthony Connolly
Died 11th March 1976
R.I.P.

Moss swore under his breath, while Finny scrambled off the wall to get a closer look. They all stood in silence. This is unbelievable, thought Finny.

'D'ye think it'd maybe be someone a bit touched in the head?' queried Jack, never at a loss.

'Perhaps,' said Moss quietly enough, but Finny whose eyes followed the strong hands saw them tremble, and wondered.

'Never thought to come by a piece of evidence like this,' Moss said at length. 'My God, who would murder a fellow, bury him, and then get a brass plate made!' He wrapped it carefully in his handkerchief. 'Better get back on the job,' he said.

That evening, Judge Raftery surveyed his tired but not unhappy son as the latter entered the parental home around midnight.

'Hard day, Finny?' he enquired, eyeing his son's disreputable trousers, which had a tear in one leg.

'Oh a bit tiring I suppose,' replied Finny, resolving to omit all reference to the wall.

The Judge nodded. 'I hear they put you with Coen,' he remarked casually.

'He tells me to call him Moss,' said Finny, with a grin.

'Treating you all right?'

'Quite decent. He doesn't yell the way old McCracken did.'

'Naturally McCracken would find your inexperience exasperating. To tell the truth, I wish you were with him now.'

'What's wrong with Coen?'

His father paused as if weighing his reply. Then he said slowly: 'There's no evidence to suggest he's not good at his job. In fact he is reputed to be very good indeed.'

'He's good all right, and thorough.'

'You like him, Finny?'

'I'd say he keeps a pretty tight lid on himself. I don't know that I'd care to be around if it ever really came off.'

The Judge regarded his son with some respect.

3

The town of Gifford, whose earliest recorded vicissitude was its seizure and occupation by the Danes in 982, had had a number of unhappy episodes in its history, and although its inhabitants viewed this latest with some revulsion, their numbers were nearly evenly divided between those who thought it would ruin their tourist image and those who felt it would bring greater business. Certainly in the short term, the latter group appeared to have taken the more correct view, for at the week-end, large numbers of the Dublin population took their wives and children to sit on Gifford's beaches and swim in Gifford waters, with a tour of the graveyard as an added attraction.

The morning after the funeral, the weather turned chilly and in the Lovell household tempers which on the previous day had been explosive following on Martin's reaction to the newspaper coverage of his daughter's presence at the inquest, had now cooled to a frigid politeness on the part of Martin and a stony silence on the part of his daughter. Matters had not been eased by the arrival of some gentlemen of the press, two from daily newspapers and a photographer. Martin having abused and scouted these gentlemen, he returned to the home front and railed against Mrs. Connolly for having had the effrontery to suggest his daughter should get mixed up in this affair, at his wife for not having stopped her anyway and at Geraldine herself for having been such a fool.

Geraldine merely raised her very fair eyebrows. 'What has you so upset? I am the one who suffered, having to say publicly that Simon didn't want me — preferred that brat Lily — much good will it do her now.'

'What you wanted with Connolly in the first place, we'll never know,' Martin snorted.

'I never wanted him,' replied his daughter rather wearily, and her voice quavered away and sank. 'I wish I were free of the whole dreary mess.'

Martin's rage having cooled, he thought the more, and the following day he phoned his solicitor. When he mentioned this fact to Geraldine, she simply stared at him and said nothing.

Shortly afterwards, there arrived at the front door of this tense household, that fledgling in the world of criminal investigation — Detective Garda Finnbarr Raftery.

'You go and try your luck with the Lovells,' Moss had said as he prepared to study the deceased's various garments and wrappings, now well documented.

Finny, astounded and trying not to show it, replied: 'What line of questioning shall I take?'

'Ask 'em anything you like,' said Moss offhandedly, 'and write down the answers.'

This was so unhelpful that Finny said no more but set out for Furry Park House with an increased heart beat. He wore a thin wool suit and carried a folded poplin coat, and his appearance so coincided with the Lovell housekeeper's idea of a member of the legal profession, that he was admitted to their elegant drawing-room under the mistaken impression that he was 'the solicitor Mr. Martin was expecting.'

Martin and Grace Lovell entered the room together, Mrs. Lovell being a slight fair-haired woman with round shoulders and thin transparent hands.

Martin gazed at Finny in some surprise. 'I was expecting Brennan himself,' he said shortly.

Finny did not know quite how to take this, and introduced himself simply as 'Raftery' accepting Mrs. Lovell's proffered hand as he did so.

Martin cocked an ear. 'No relation to Judge Raftery, I suppose?'

'His son,' replied Finny modestly.

Martin thawed and pulled up a chair. 'Brennan probably knows what he's doing,' he said. 'Now this,' he continued in a confidential tone, 'this is a very delicate matter.'

'Yes,' said Finny, encouragingly, and taking out a large notebook. He wrote an introductory note. Really the whole thing was going to be so much easier than he could have imagined.

Martin viewed the notebook with approval. 'I suppose you saw the picture in the newspapers?' he queried, 'of Geraldine I mean.'

'Oh yes,' said Finny.

'If I had had anything to do with it, that would never have happened. Didn't know until it was all over.'

'A pity,' said Finny involuntarily.

Mrs. Lovell said: 'It's terrible to think of our Geraldine mixed up in this and it's not as if she were still Simon's fiancée. That had all ended before he went away.'

Finny coughed and said (he had a burning curiosity to know): 'How was it broken off so suddenly?'

'He threw her over,' Martin growled.

'Surely not?'

Mrs. Lovell warmed to this nice young man. 'Geraldine is very beautiful, isn't she?'

'She's lovely,' replied Finny with sincerity.

Martin said, still in the confidential tone he had previously used: 'We thought it strange, I can tell you, but then she never confided in us. We didn't like Connolly and we think she just took him to spite us.'

'Why would she do that?'

'Well dear,' Mrs. Lovell forestalled an explosive sound from her spouse, and turned towards him apologetically, 'well, Mr. Lovell said so much against him you see, right from the start, it hurt Geraldine I think.'

'She's sensitive then?'

'No, not sensitive exactly,' her mother was rather at a loss, but Martin chipped in with a grin:

'Obstinate as a mule,' he said, 'oh yes, takes after Grace's father, the old — He was a tartar. Couldn't stand the sight of me. Didn't want Grace to have me. Thought I was a poor match for her. That was why . . . ' he broke off, and Finny intuitively nodded.

Mrs. Lovell took one of her husband's hands and squeezed it. 'We want to protect Geraldine as much as possible,' she said anxiously.

'Quite natural,' said Finny. 'What was Simon Connolly like?'

Again Martin would have replied but Grace Lovell said at once: 'He was a fine-looking fellow. I think that's why Geraldine was so taken with him at first.'

'He was a chancer,' Martin said, 'a no-good chancer.'

Grace laughed softly. 'You know dear that's just what my father used to say about you.'

Martin turned to her indignantly. 'I was always honest, well, reasonably honest anyhow.'

'You think Connolly wasn't?' Finny was so interested, his questions formed themselves.

'We don't know that he was actually dishonest, do we dear?' Grace said.

'I know the type, and in the event I was right. Look how he treated Geraldine. Here today and gone tomorrow.'

'But you really don't know why?' persisted Finny.

'She wouldn't tell us.'

'Was she upset?'

Her mother nodded and made an expressive movement with her long thin hands. 'At first she seemed to take it well enough. I suppose it was shock really. After a while though, she became very depressed. However, she seems to have got over it completely, or had at least until this happened, and even now she has stood up to the ordeal of the inquest and she never mentioned it to her father or myself until we read of it in the papers. Indeed, but for Mrs. Connolly she need never have been there. That woman had no right whatever to ask Geraldine to go with her. He was her son, and not connected with us in any way.' Mrs. Lovell's voice rose and her husband put his arm around her shoulders.

'Can't be helped now,' he said.

'What about Lily Sullivan?' queried Finny.

'Hardly knew her,' said Martin.

'Oh I did,' responded his wife with more animation. She regarded Finny with a little twisted smile. 'You will think me catty, I'm afraid,' she said.

'Tell me,' Finny said, grinning.

'Well she had a certain type of bold good looks, and rather a sharp tongue. I don't know why Miss Purcell tolerated her. Still, Lily always struck me as being pretty efficient, so I suppose her employer didn't want to lose her.'

'Was she very young?'

'About twenty or so, but she could look older sometimes.'

'And how old is Geraldine?'

'Eighteen — will be nineteen in August.'

Finny hesitated, then got up his courage. 'Perhaps I might have a word with her now, if she is at home?'

Martin and Grace looked at one another.

'She's out, as a matter of fact,' said Grace soothingly, 'gone up to town for the day.'

'Oh I see,' said Finny, closing his notebook. 'I'll be on my way so.'

Martin took him to the door and stood there while Finny walked to the end of the long tarmac driveway, with its two expensive cars parked side by side near the house.

Hardly had the door closed behind him when the subject of this conversation emerged from a room at the head of the stairs.

'Well, what did he want?' she asked sharply, 'I thought you had the solicitor with you.'

'Brennan sent this fellow in his place. Quite pleasant I must say.'

'Brennan sent him!' she repeated, 'you must be mad. I saw him three days ago at the inquest and he was pointed out to me as Inspector Coen's assistant, Detective Raftery!'

It was not to be supposed that the atmosphere in the Lovell home was improved by this piece of information, and brushing aside all protestations of incredulity, ignorance and sheer helplessness, Miss Lovell again retired to her room, slamming the door and shouting that they would be the death of her.

Happily unaware of this state of affairs, Finny went on his way and wrote up a nice report for Moss which the latter read with some amazement.

'They told you all this?'

'Yes,' said Finny, trying to conceal his satisfaction.

Moss ruffled up his hair. 'Some of this stuff might fit in with a theory of mine, but why were they so frank about it, if it is frankness, that is?' He sounded worried. 'We'll have to get on with this business of Lily Sullivan,' he said.

Gifford's sub-post office is in New Terrace, known to the local population as Coltsfoot Lane. To this place, Moss directed his steps, passing a row of thatched cottages, and beyond them Sir Mortimer ffrench's house and gardens open to the public Wednesdays and Saturdays. Turning into Coltsfoot Lane, he found a number of small shops and in their midst one with 'Purcell' written in old-fashioned lettering above the door, which was shut.

Lifting the latch, he went in, the step down taking him by surprise. A bell rang as the door opened and from behind a curtained grille a young woman came into view, wearing large black-rimmed glasses.

The shop was divided into two sections, the post office side being severely functional, while opposite a variety of stationery goods and souvenirs were displayed at one end together with some china and glass, and at the other a glass topped counter held stocks of knitting wool. Wool also filled shelves at the back of the counter, and in addition some hand-knitted garments were set out on stands. The floor of the shop was covered in hardwearing lino, while at the goods counter a piece of coconut matting and a spoonbacked chair invited the prospective customer.

Moss was reflecting that quite a number of years had passed since he was last inside premises of this description, when the proprietress emerged. Miss Mary Purcell was forty-seven years of age, plain looking and with straight features and a strong chin. Her hair, which was only slightly grey, she wore combed back and held in a tortoiseshell clasp. On this occasion, she was clad in a hand-knitted jumper and skirt of a moderately fashionable shape, and pinned to the brown jumper was a really beautiful gold brooch in a celtic design.

'I'm Inspector Coen,' said Moss, 'and I'd be glad if you would answer one or two questions.'

His glance took in the bespectacled girl, and Miss Purcell nodded and said perhaps he would come through to the fire inside. She led the way through the back door of the shop and he found himself in a small sitting-room, over-crowded with mahogany furniture, and heated by a flaring gas fire. Miss Purcell indicated a high-backed armchair beside the fire and Moss wasted no time in coming to the point.

'I want to know about Lily Sullivan,' he said, 'and in particular if you have had any letters from her since she left here in February.'

The postmistress went over to a small desk. 'Lily wrote to me twice,' she said. 'As soon as I heard what had been said at the inquest, I knew these would be wanted.'

She gave them to him and he opened one. It was brief to the point of curtness. Dated February 19th, it said the writer was having some difficulty in getting a suitable job and would be glad if Miss Purcell would forward a reference, as quickly as possible, and also any mail. But the next was more helpful. Sent on March 5th, Lily asked that no letters be forwarded for the present as Simon was going home to Gifford for a few days and would call to the shop to collect anything for her.

'Did he call here?'

Mary Purcell seated herself on a red plush stool, crossed her legs and smoothed down the folds of her skirt.

'No,' she said.

'Did any letters come for her?'

'One only, and that had already been re-forwarded before her last letter came.'

'Was it a personal letter, do you remember?'

For the first time during their conversation, Miss Purcell paused uncertainly.

She's read it, thought Moss. He would have to tread warily. 'You felt yourself responsible for her?' he actually said.

She looked straight at him, and he tried again:

'You were in a difficult position of course,' he prompted.

Her reaction surprised him. 'You think I read it?' she exclaimed, and then, without waiting for an answer she suddenly capitulated: 'Well,' she said bluntly, 'as a matter of fact I did!'

'What was in it?' His relief showed, and her reply came with a rush.

'It was from Mrs. Sullivan, Lily's mother. It said they had not heard from her since Christmas and they were a bit worried, as she hadn't answered their two previous letters. It said to write straight away and let them know how she was.'

'What day was this?'

'It was the day before I got hers I think,' Miss Purcell was regaining her natural poise now. 'I did feel responsible,' she added briskly, 'and when I had looked up the directory and found they were on the phone, I rang through and asked to speak to her mother.'

Moss could hardly credit this piece of luck. 'What did she say?'

'Well, first of all I said the letter had been opened in the rush of mail here. I don't suppose Mrs. Sullivan believed me but she spoke very nicely, and I said how Lily had left the month before to go to Manchester. I gave her the address and she thanked me warmly, so much so I believe she had been really anxious.'

'I should like the Sullivans' address,' said Moss, taking out a piece of paper.

'It's not far from Limerick city; Ballach-Larkin.'

'Right,' said Moss, 'I'm very much obliged for this information. What about Lily herself? What kind of girl is she?'

Mary Purcell seemed a little reluctant. 'She was a good worker,' she said at last. 'We didn't always get along too well, but in spite of that I liked her.'

'Could I ask what you thought of Simon Connolly?'

'I hardly knew him.'

'The last report we received suggested he might be dishonest. Was he?'

Miss Purcell seemed genuinely surprised.

'I don't know who would have suggested such a thing,' she said, 'his father was one of the best liked people in the town and Mrs. Connolly is a very nice person. In fact, I have never heard of anything against that family.'

'Right,' said Moss, 'as I've said, I'm

obliged for all you've told me, and it is of course entirely in confidence.'

Mary Purcell gave him a direct look.

When Moss got back to the station, it was to find the police report on Lily Sullivan just come in. It said enquiries had ascertained that on the 26th March she had vacated her room at the Manchester address. She had packed up her belongings and had left by taxi; destination and present whereabouts unknown.

4

When the Inspector next went in search of information he trod the same path as previously to Miss Purcell's shop. However, instead of turning off at the ffrench estate, he carried on up the hill road which led inland and which, after a quarter of a mile or so, brought him to Moy Farm, the Connolly home. The farmhouse was a modest two storey building of modern design. A black and white collie dog sat on the front step and growled warningly as Moss approached.

The front door opened and a man came out. He was tall and lean and Moss remembered seeing him with Mrs. Connolly on the day of the funeral. The dog jumped up and pawed the man affectionately, and the man stepped backwards, grinning.

'I suppose I'd better let him in,' he said. At the last word, the dog bounded past him into the hallway, after which a loud exclamation of dismay proclaimed his arrival in the kitchen.

Mrs. Connolly came out into the hall. 'Oh Owen, what did you let him in for?'

'He'll be off up the fields, Maggie, rounding up the cattle. I caught him at it yesterday when the McLaughlins came.'

Mrs. Connolly smiled apologetically at Moss, and the latter stepped into the hall.

'He likes to show off to strangers,' she said, patting the dog who gazed up at her adoringly. 'We don't keep sheep now, but if he got the chance he'd collect every beast we have and pack them into the front field there, just to show he can do it.' She paused, then said: 'You've come about our poor Simon of course,' her voice held a sigh. 'Come into the front room here and sit down.' She stood aside for him to pass, her face set in resignation. Owen followed her into the small sparsely furnished room.

It seemed natural to her to shed tears and hardly had she seated herself than she began to cry. Owen's arm went round her shoulders.

'Maggie,' he said, 'the Inspector wants

to know all about Simon and we have to tell him as much as we can.' He sat on the arm of her chair, still holding her, and looked at Moss.

'She's been through a bad time. By the way, I'm Owen Connolly — a cousin of the family.'

Moss said conversationally: 'I've already had a few words with a Mr. McClintock.'

Mrs. Connolly exclaimed: 'He never called to see us!'

'I believe he mentioned he didn't want to intrude.'

'It was very good of him to come,' she went on seriously, 'he can scarcely ever bring himself to leave the farm — it's his whole life.'

'Even as a boy he was like that,' Owen agreed. 'I remember spending summers with them — his father was alive at the time — and Terry fairly ran things himself, and the father was glad to let him, for a bit of peace I think.'

'He never married of course,' Mrs. Connolly murmured regretfully.

Moss was pleased to let the conversation take this turn. 'I left him talking to

Rachel Payne; he was asking her about the family in New Zealand.'

Mrs. Connolly was diverted at once, but Owen said: 'You came to ask about Simon, didn't you?'

Moss said soothingly: 'If you can tell me what I need to know, I have no wish to distress Mrs. Connolly.'

'No, no,' she said fretfully, 'it's only right. After all, I'm his mother.'

'Why did your son go to England, Mrs. Connolly?'

She flushed and said defensively: 'He'd got engaged and they wanted to save up to get married.'

'From the evidence at the inquest, it appears he had already been engaged to another young woman without any desire to go away to make money?'

She looked positively flustered. 'Oh yes, Geraldine. Of course that was a different affair altogether. Mr. Lovell is very well-to-do.'

'Did he approve of the match?'

'At first, no, he didn't, but I think Geraldine talked him round. We were invited to the house in August, I think it was,' she looked a little helplessly at Owen, 'just a small party to celebrate the engagement.'

'Had your son given his fiancée an engagement ring?'

'Oh yes, it was a very nice one. He had to spend all his savings to buy it.'

'And borrow some,' Owen added drily.

'What happened to it?'

'Why he . . . ' she broke off and Owen gave a rather twisted smile and then said: 'We never saw it again of course, but I should say it was the same one he afterwards gave Lily.'

'What was the reason for the broken engagement?'

'I don't really know, Inspector,' Mrs. Connolly sounded genuinely ignorant. 'He came in one day and said they weren't going to get married after all and he wouldn't give a reason. And then, several days later, he told us he was going to marry Lily instead.'

'When did Simon actually leave here?'

'I've been trying to remember — February 10th, perhaps.'

'That's very useful,' replied Moss,

writing down the information.

Mrs. Connolly seemed to relax, and Owen smiled at her. Suddenly the door opened and three people crowded into the room, only stopping when they saw the stranger. Their mother rose awkwardly to her feet.

'This is Brendan, my boy,' she put a rather fiercely protective arm round him, 'and these are my daughters, Dorothy and Anne.'

'Just one more question,' Moss said, 'particularly since the whole family is present. Did any of you see or speak to or hear from Simon after you received the letter from him dated March 3rd?'

'Have you found any traces of him after that date?' asked Owen.

'Not really,' Moss replied, and they all earnestly assured him that no one had seen or heard from him since.

However, if the Connollys were anxious to assist the police, the same could not be said of the Sullivan family, as Sergeant O'Shea discovered after a long journey south. It was no part of his duties to undertake detective work, but he had volunteered, and the Superintendent had given it his blessing. Before long, O'Shea began to regret his initiative.

Mr. Sullivan, a tall rough-spoken man, said bluntly they could do without prying into their family affairs. Lily was in England, minding her own business. If her fiancé got himself murdered, always supposing it was murder, what was that to do with her? Let the police get on with finding out who killed him and let decent people mind their own affairs in peace.

Ellen Sullivan, Lily's mother, a tall handsome woman with a great quantity of dark hair swept up on top of her head and a bold countenance which put the Sergeant in mind of Lily's description, was as uncooperative as her husband, if rather more polite. Yes, she had received a phone call from Miss Purcell — a kindly spoken person. Yes, she had been in contact with Lily at that time, and Lily had written saying she was thinking of moving. No, they did not have her present address, but if she should write, of course they would let her know the police were anxious to interview her. Unfortunately, her previous letter had been burnt or thrown out, otherwise they would gladly have shown it to the Sergeant. There was no mystery about Lily. Many young girls went to England to work, and moved from place to place.

The Sergeant dutifully interviewed Lily's three brothers without result, except that the youngest, who was a mechanic at the local garage, said it was a shame Lily should be mixed up in this, and that Simon Connolly was no good to her anyway. When asked to expound on this statement, he shut up completely on the subject, and abused the Sergeant instead.

A disappointed O'Shea was on the point of departure, when an old lady hobbled into the police station and asked to see him. Even on this warm June day, she wore a good black coat and hat.

'I'm Mrs. Crotty,' she said by way of introduction. She was all at once breathless, flustered and upset. 'I don't really know that I should be here at all,' she added.

He pulled out a chair for her, into

which she lowered herself cautiously. The local man on duty went outside, and Mrs. Crotty breathed what might have been a sigh of relief.

'You wanted to tell me something?' O'Shea asked.

But she was not yet ready for that. 'My grandson works at the garage, you see, and he came out to tell me what had been said.'

'You are Lily's grandmother?'

'Aye, indeed. Twenty grandchildren I have, and three great-grandchildren.' Her breath was easier now.

'You wanted to tell me something about Lily?' he prompted.

'What will you do if you don't find her?'

'The police in England are looking for her now.'

'Dear, dear,' cried Mrs. Crotty vexedly, 'was ever a thing more unfortunate! Tell me,' she turned to him earnestly, 'why must you find her?'

'Because she is the last person we know of who saw Simon Connolly alive, and we want her to tell us about it.'

She looked up into his face as if searching for an answer to her problems, and was apparently reassured, for she said at length: 'If she wrote to you, would that do?'

'Do you know where she is?'

'I make no promises mind, but if she were to write you, I could send on the letter.'

The Sergeant decided to risk giving offence. 'Am I to take it, ma'am, ye're to have another great-grandchild?'

She nodded: 'Now you see why we've to be careful. If it gets known, the family'd be ruined.'

The Sergeant, who understood that point of view well enough, said: 'But surely this happens from time to time, even in a place like Ballach-Larkin?'

'Sure it does,' she agreed, 'but those that can, keep it well hid. You'll not find her, but you'll disgrace her with looking.'

The Sergeant tried another ploy: 'Social Welfare people can be very discreet,' he said.

Mrs. Crotty dismissed the Department of Social Welfare with a gesture of her arthritic hand, and O'Shea decided to take what he could get.

'Let her write what she knows,' he said. 'Everything about Simon during the last days he was with her; particularly about why he decided to return home and when exactly he left her.'

'I'll do that,' she promised, 'and you'll stop looking for her, will you?'

This was a good deal more than the Sergeant could agree to. 'I'll tell the Inspector what you've told me,' he murmured confidentially. 'He's not a hard man, and only wants to get at the truth. Maybe when he sees the letter, it will satisfy him.'

'I'll do it then,' she said, 'sure it can do Lily no harm anyway.'

She pressed his hand between her two stiff-jointed ones, and then hobbled out of the station.

5

Moss woke around six. The curtains had been left apart and as his narrow bed faced the small and uncomfortable back window of the O'Shea cottage, the strong early morning sun blazed directly on his face. He got out of bed and looked out of the window which gave a sea view of sorts between two parallel streets sloping towards the beach. He decided he would go for a short walk.

Dressed in shirt and slacks and with a poplin coat, for the bright sun belied the sharp cold of the early morning, he headed for the beach, passing down the almost deserted principal street as he did so. He turned off by the side of the public library, and made his way along Ship Street. He did not go down to the harbour but turned to the right and took a narrow path leading to the sandy beach. There was no wind and the sun rising higher and losing its red tinge warmed him as he walked by the water's edge, his feet sinking a little in the damp soft sand, for the tide was going out.

Standing and looking out to sea, he forgot Simon Connolly's dead body and its attendant mysteries. He remembered only that he had not yet swum in Gifford's tranquil waters. He gazed around, but the beach was empty. He bent down and removed his shoes and socks and rolled up the ends of his slacks.

Shoes in hand, he stepped forward a little and the gentle waves lapped over his feet. He looked round again. If he were going to disrobe, he would have to do it publicly for Gifford's beach was innocent of bathing huts or even a sheltering rock. Well, there was no one to see apparently.

He removed almost all his garments and placed them in a neat bundle with the shoes and his watch, wrapping the whole in his poplin coat and putting it several yards from the receding tide. That done, he flung himself into the sea. The strength of his strokes carried him out into deep water, and he turned and swam parallel with the beach for some time.

After half an hour or so, he decided he had had enough and made to return to his belongings. His eyes scanned the shore without recognition until he remembered about the departing tide and directed his gaze further inland. But there was nothing!

He came up out of the water and after a short search found the spot where his bundle should have reposed. It was readily identifiable by the fact that a pair of long slim footprints now led away from it, mingling with his own deeper ones for a few yards and then solitarily making their way along the water's edge in the direction of the harbour.

Away to his left, three prospective bathers had appeared and were running up and down, their shouts carrying on the clear still air. He looked down at his underpants, and a glimmer of humour showed in the usually cold, very blue eyes. Retiring to the water, he swam along following the footprints until they reached the outside of the harbour wall. Here they went down into the water and disappeared. He felt the strong current around him, and wondered. The harbour wall towered above, some forty feet high, and his eyes ran along its course out to sea, stopping at the iron girder which ran up the entire height of the wall and over the top.

He swam over to the wall, reached out to the rail, and began to climb. When he finally reached the top, he paused and looked over. The harbour presented a deserted aspect, the fishing fleet being away out to sea at this hour. The yachts and small boats were tucked away close by the jetty. A solitary small boy with a home-made fishing rod sat with it at the end of the pier and gazed intently into the water.

Moss viewed with some interest three or four sheds close by, the door of the first being invitingly ajar. He got down and moved towards it. No one was there. A small window gave some dim light to the interior which was crammed with fishing gear of all kinds, and on a rough wooden bench near the door was a coat of a familiar hue. He searched for the other clothes without success, and finally he buttoned on the coat and went out to speak to the small angler.

As he approached, he gave a short cough and the boy turned round and gave him a close scrutiny.

'I'm looking for some clothes,' remarked Moss, without heat.

The boy nodded seriously. 'She has them for you, she said to tell you.'

If the Inspector was surprised, he did not show it. 'Where?' he said.

'Over there in the yacht — see the one that's got the blue stripe along the side — the *Elmer*.'

For a moment it seemed as if Moss would have questioned him, but then the detective turned and with his coat flapping around his bare legs made his way along the pier. The water being low, he climbed down an iron ladder to where five or six small boats were moored together, clambering from one to the next until the yellow and white yacht was in front of him.

He grabbed hold of the handrail and pulled himself on board to meet Miss Lovell emerging from the cabin in sweater and shorts. She was, he immediately perceived, in a very tense condition easily productive of tantrums or tears, and he slid a mental chunk of ice across his own annoyance.

'You took my stuff?' he enquired matter-of-factly.

This attitude she had clearly not expected. 'It's in the cabin,' and she waved a vague hand in that direction.

'Excuse me a moment,' he replied and descended the three steps. Here the remainder of his garments were neatly laid, and after a search for his watch he found it in a trouser pocket. It did not appear to have been in the water and he put it on with something like gratitude.

Respectably clad, he re-emerged to find Miss Lovell seated in the stern and swinging a nonchalant leg over the side. As he came near, she swung round to face him, not without some nervousness, he thought.

'I suppose you're pretty mad at me,' she said, and then, as he made no response, 'look, about Simon, I don't know what impression my parents gave your . . . er assistant, the other day. The whole thing was a stupid mistake. He got into the house under false pretences.'

If she had intended to divert him at once, she could hardly have hoped for better success.

'Raftery!' Moss was frankly astounded.

'I don't say he did it deliberately,' she conceded. 'Dad was expecting the family solicitor and this fellow turned up instead and they thought you see . . . ' she broke off, then went on with new vigour: 'He told them he was a judge's son or something, and so of course they thought our solicitor had sent him in his place.'

She looked up and met the very cold blue eyes.

'Well, anyway,' she continued, getting up and moving round restlessly, 'they gave him a whole load of details they never would have if, well, you know . . . I don't even know what they said to him,' she burst out, 'I shouted at them so much, now they won't speak to me.'

At that moment, Moss Coen took a liking to Geraldine Lovell which he never afterwards lost, despite what was to follow. He seated himself on the side of the boat and the next time she passed him in her aimless wanderings, took her firmly by the arm and pushed her down beside him.

'Now,' he said, 'I'm not Raftery. You tell me about Simon and yourself.'

'He was a louse,' she said flatly.

'Because he gave you up?'

'I didn't care about that. It would have come to an end soon enough.' The disinterest in her voice persuaded him she spoke the truth.

'What about Lily?' he prompted.

She looked at him rather more coolly. 'You haven't been able to find her, have you?'

'Why, do you think something could have happened to her?'

Geraldine seemed quite genuinely surprised. 'Lily is fully capable of taking care of herself,' she replied firmly.

'You didn't like her?'

'She wasn't my type.'

Moss tried another tack. 'Did anyone around these parts hate Simon enough to kill him?' He thought she might have balked at that one, but her answer came readily enough.

'No one ever hated Simon. He didn't arouse the emotions. Even now, I couldn't hate him.' She turned away and looked out to sea. 'He's dead anyway,' she added, 'what difference does it make?'

'Believe me,' he replied, half smiling, 'it makes a difference.'

'What will you do if you can't find out what happened to him, or why he was killed?'

'I'll do my best to find out,' he responded with emphasis. 'This your boat?' he added rather rudely.

'Dad's,' she replied. 'Of course I have the use of it.'

'Nice for you.'

'Envious?' she queried sweetly.

'Let's get back to the matter in hand — Simon. Any ideas on why he came back here?'

'He never shared any secrets with me.'

'What about the ring?' he asked abruptly.

'What ring?'

'The engagement ring. I was told you

had one. Did you give it back?'

She grinned at him and jumped up, making an extravagant gesture with her arm, as if flinging an imaginary ring into the water.

'I returned it,' she said, and laughed. 'He asked me for it anyway.'

'When did he ask you?'

'Oh, I don't know. Some time before he left.'

'Did he give it to Lily?'

He heard her catch her breath. 'You mean to hurt, don't you,' she said.

'I mean to get at the truth.'

'Well,' she went on viciously, 'if he gave it to Lily, it would have had to be altered. Her hands are twice my size,' and she held out long slim delicate hands for his inspection. He caught at one of them and felt her instinctive tug away from him, and the strength of it.

He looked at his watch. 'I'd better get back. I suppose half of Gifford has seen us here by now.'

'Does that bother you?'

'In my profession? Hardly.' He paused and then said diffidently: 'Look I'm sorry if I said anything to upset you. In this job one stops feeling human at times.'

She smiled quite readily. 'Sure thing,' she said. 'Don't worry about me.'

Strangely enough, he did, as he walked back along the pier. The little boy was gone and with him the early morning yachtsmen, and the harbour was deserted once more. At the corner of Ship Street, he stopped in his tracks and turned to look back to the boats. But the *Elmer* was no longer there. With a spinnaker hoisted, she slowly passed the rows of small yachts and rowing boats and even as he watched she reached the harbour mouth and disappeared from view.

He turned and walked up Ship Street, whose shops were beginning to open and he thought about the interview just concluded. She hadn't told him much he didn't know already, or that her parents hadn't told Raftery if it came to that. So why had she wanted to speak to him, so urgently she would decoy him to a spot of her own choosing?

Why indeed? But she had let fall one piece of interesting information. The question was, could it be genuine, or had she in fact deliberately planted it for him to pick up. She was so nervous too. Eighteen-year-olds were often nervous, but she had been cool at the inquest and now cool enough to climb a forty foot wall. Better not to put too much stress on any part of the whole affair then.

It was perhaps fortunate for the Inspector's peace of mind that he could not know of a 'development' to take place later in the day, involving the subject of his recent interview and that other thorn in the flesh, Finnbarr Raftery.

6

Finny was patronising one of Gifford's few night spots. Its rather garish decoration was softened by dim lighting, so dim in fact that it was difficult to recognise anyone more distant than eight or nine paces, but with that curious instinct which comes to a man in Finny's emotional state, the first person whom he saw, sitting on a stool at the bar, and dressed in silky green turquoise, was Geraldine Lovell.

Her long hair, which at the inquest she had worn perfectly straight and tied at the back, was now fluffed and hung round her face in soft curls, and the colours of her make-up blended with her dress. Finny Raftery thought he had never seen a girl so lovely. Since the stage was the only brightly lit part of the room, he came within hailing distance of his vision unobserved, even had he imagined she would recognise him. The conversation around her became audible.

' . . . took his car past and let it rip.'

'Murty will be killed one of these days.'

'He's never very drunk — Gerry you're never drunk anyway.'

'Who says I've never been drunk?'

''Course she has. Remember . . . '

'Shut up. Who asked you?'

'No offence, sweet one.'

'Why are we sitting here?'

'I'd ask you to partner me, heart's delight, if a gombeen of a Blackrock man hadn't blacked my ankle on Saturday. The wounds have yet to heal.'

'Rugby is such a coarse game.'

'Don't mind him — the squash fanatic.'

Finny quietly ordered himself a drink. Miss Lovell's glass needed refilling, and her rugby playing escort ordered another vodka. The squash player had lager. After a while, she got up to dance taking the squash player with her. He was a perfect athletic specimen with good white teeth, and Finny heartily despised him. The fellow with the swollen ankle he thought he knew, and when the other two had disappeared into the gloom, he slid himself and his drink along the bar counter and sat next to the rugby player.

It was quite some time since he had met him — University he thought it was — and at first the name refused to come. Finally the fellow turned round to look at the dance floor and Finny said suddenly:

'Kevin Flynn!'

'Oh hi, who are you — wait, it's coming — I know your face. Oh, got it; Finny something.'

'Bang on,' replied Finny laughing, 'Raftery.'

'Oh yes, of course. Well, how are you me old flower?'

'Poor old nose to the grindstone.'

'What at? Law, wasn't it?'

'I gave it up when I got my degree. Joined the police instead. What are you doing yourself?'

'Dad wants me to join the business of course. So far I've managed to put him off. Every time I go to the office, it takes them a week to recover. It got a bit tiresome for a while and he threatened to cut off supplies unless I 'knuckled down' as he put it. I countered that threat with some bravura of my own though.'

'What did you do?' enquired Finny, amused.

'Talked about emigrating to South America. Some place where they're always having revolutions, so it sounded suitably dangerous.'

'And did he believe you?'

'No. The trouble with being the only son is that the parents get to know you too well. However, to show I meant business, I went through all the formalities. Could go tomorrow if I wanted to, and if I had the money,' he finished gloomily.

'What are you hoping for — a win on the nags?'

Finny's companion brightened up. 'Never know your luck. Seriously though, I got an offer from an international company out there, looking for graduates. They'd pay the fare out if I'd contract with them for two years.'

'Two years is a long time. What about your friend?' he indicated the dance floor.

'Which one?'

Finny grinned. 'The pretty one.'

His companion gazed in the general direction of the dancers and then turned and morosely regarded his drink.

'Yes — well that's as may be,' he said. 'Honestly Finny, she's a good looker all right, and plenty of the ready too — at least her dad has. I tell you my old man was simply thrilled when he heard about her. Now I don't know what to do.'

'How's that?'

'Come off it, and you in the Gardai. Surely you know who she is. She's the girl who's mixed up in the murder case here — her ex-fiancé got himself done-in and quietly buried.'

'Nothing to do with her, surely?'

'Oh you know how people talk. It seems a rotten thing to say, but one has to use the old head. A pity because . . . well, I was hanging in there with a good chance, and now . . . ' he broke off.

Finny's anger rose against his erstwhile friend. He could have hit the fellow, now silent and brooding over his drink. Hot words trembled on his lips, but were never uttered. The fellow's a fool, he thought. And what of himself? Would

Geraldine even look twice at him. Still, his opportunity was now.

'Who's your friend?' asked a voice behind them, and both turned round to find the subject of their thoughts had returned with the squash player. She was fanning herself vigorously with her hand and there were beads of sweat on her forehead. 'Give me a drink quick; something on the rocks.'

Finny was introduced as Kevin's friend from way back. She made no sign of recognition, and he ordered drinks for all four. Geraldine dived into a pocket in the folds of her dress and produced a minuscule handkerchief and tiny make-up repair equipment. As they waited for their drinks, she doctored her face using the bar mirror, and Finny who sat on her left, hardly took his eyes from her reflection, while continuing his conversation with Kevin. This largely consisted of 'do you remembers?' and when the drinks came, Geraldine said she had heard enough and to stop boring her.

'Dance this one with me?' Finny said.

She regarded him sideways under her

lashes, heavy with mascara, and a little smile softened her mouth. 'Would the Inspector approve?' she whispered. The perfume she used had the fragrance of roses.

'I'm not on duty.'

She got up and glided away ahead of him. His mind focused on his feet (his shoes were size elevens) and he determined to keep them out of her way. He was not naturally clumsy but her delicate slimness affected his nerves. She danced well of course and he stomped round her not too unhappily. Finny essayed some desultory conversation but the five man group effectively drowned out all other sound. Eventually she pulled at his arm and led him back to the bar.

'I'm tired,' she said dismissively, picking up her drink and finishing it in one gulp. 'I'm going home.'

'The night is young, sweet one. Kevin and I rather fancied another hour or so, didn't we?'

Kevin got up slowly. 'Sorry, Gerry, I'll run you home of course,' but he looked speculatively at Finny.

'I'll take you home,' said the latter, 'if you don't mind walking that is.'

The squash player burst out laughing. 'You've nerve, boy, I'll say that for you. Sweetie here wouldn't walk a step — she even came without a coat.'

'Oh shut up Cormac, I'm going anyway,' and she suited her actions to the words.

Neither of the two young men moved, and Finny said: 'I'll get my coat, it's not far to her house.' He shook hands with Kevin and said they must get together soon, nodded to Cormac, and left abruptly.

By the time he had reclaimed his coat, she had left the hall and he looked for her in the street outside. She was a good distance ahead, the light from the street lamps picking up the shimmer of her green dress. He broke into a run, his long legs sprinting forward, and in a few minutes he had overtaken her. He put the coat round her shoulders, although the night was still fairly warm. She looked at it disdainfully.

'This is almost the same as the

Inspector's. Regulation police issue?'

He ignored the sarcasm. 'No,' he said, 'we wear our own clothes.'

'I suppose he told you about this morning.'

'What about?' Finny asked warily.

'Oh never mind. It was all a mistake anyhow. I told him that.'

'Honestly, I haven't a clue what you're talking about!'

'You don't seem to have much of a clue about anything. Fancy not having a car!'

'Can't afford it yet.'

'Are you very poor?'

'Just about break even.'

'My parents told me you said your father was a judge or something — was that the truth?'

'Yes, I'm Judge Raftery's son. He's retired of course, and anyway I don't live on him.'

'Meaning I live on my Dad. Why shouldn't I? He likes it that way, and he's going to buy me a car too, so . . . ' The last hastily swallowed drink, combined with sudden fresh air, was producing a rather unfortunate result, and she trailed out to the edge of the path and caught hold of a small tree.

The next step seemed quite natural to him, he had such long arms. He came over behind her and put one round her shoulders. Then he stooped down and lifted her legs off the ground. She went rigid for a moment, and then relaxed.

'I'll be your car,' he said, smiling down at her.

'I'm not sloshed, am I?'

'A bit,' he admitted.

'That's since Simon. Always getting sloshed now. Why I don't know. Never cared for him. He's better off dead anyhow.'

'I'm the policeman, remember,' he said warningly.

'It doesn't matter, nothing does any more.'

'Soon be home now.'

She began to cry, softly at first and then more noisily so that he looked around uneasily. The street was almost deserted, but he still had some little way to go. Also, her slim build belied her weight, for she was quite tall.

'Don't cry,' he said urgently. 'People

will think you're being assaulted or something, and I'll be drummed out of the force.'

He seemed to have said the right thing, for she stopped crying and began to laugh instead. Then he heard the sound of a car pulling in behind him. The driver blew his horn and Finny looked round to find a concerned gentleman getting out and coming over to him.

'Is the girl ill?' asked the man anxiously.

'She's not too well,' Finny replied truthfully. 'I'm taking her home — it's just up the road.'

'Get in,' said the man. 'You should have flagged me down. She's no lightweight, I'd say,' this studying Miss Lovell's form in a prosaic manner.

Finny, whose arms were indeed beginning to ache, laid his burden down in the back of the man's car. She roused up a little and the man turned and said soothingly: 'No need to worry, miss, we'll have you home in no time at all.'

Finny now saw himself having to furnish explanations to the Lovell household — an embarrassing circumstance in view of his official position. However, as it transpired, Martin and Grace Lovell were out. The housekeeper was apparently out too, or had gone to bed, and repeated ringing at the front door brought no response.

'Perhaps the young woman has a key?' suggested the driver of the car, eager to be on his way.

When roused up to search for this article, Miss Lovell hunted in her dress pocket and finally produced it. The man opened the door, while Finny assisted the lady out of the car and supported her steps into the house. He looked anxiously at his protégée whose condition seemed to be deteriorating. Now that she was in her own home, his greater preoccupation was to see her safely disposed, and leave at the earliest possible moment, before the return of her parents and awkward explanations were called for.

Coffee, that was the thing. Strong coffee. He found his way to the kitchen and turned on the light. When the coffee was ready, he tasted the result, approved of it and carried it through to the sitting-room. Geraldine was lying very quietly, and looked pale under her make-up.

'Come on,' he said, a little roughly, 'sit up and drink this.'

He took her hand, and was alarmed to discover that it was very cold. He rubbed at it feverishly, and then at the other hand. Her forehead looked damp, and she gave a little moan. He took out a handkerchief and patted her forehead, and she turned sideways and her eyes opened.

'Going to be sick,' she muttered.

He fairly dashed back into the kitchen and returned in a minute with basin and towels. Her eyes were still open but their glazed look unnerved him. 'Got to get you up on your feet,' he said, 'up with you now.'

He reached over the couch and pulled her up, supporting her back and letting her feet drop on to the floor. She hung in his arms a dead weight, and her feet trailed as he tried to make her walk. Presently he desisted and laid her back on the couch. Her eyes opened.

'No one in?' she whispered. 'Mum and Dad . . . went to the club.' Her breath was shallow and her speech short and jerky, and her overall condition such as to make him uneasy.

'Gerry, what did you have to drink?'

'Some vodkas . . . a sherry.'

'How many vodkas?'

'Three . . . four.'

'Anything else?' he shook her, 'Gerry tell me!'

'Pills,' her voice sounded far away, and she lay back on the couch.

'I'm going to phone the hospital,' he said. He went out to the hall and telephoned. Then he rang the golf club. When he came back he found she had been sick. 'You'll feel better now,' he said soothingly. She did not respond.

He sat with her until the ambulance came, and when they arrived at the hospital, her mother and father were already waiting. They took her into the casualty section and Martin went in to speak to the doctor. After a moment, he came out again and came across to Finny, who had been having a quiet word with Grace Lovell.

'They want to talk to you, young man,' Martin said heavily, 'and when they've done, I've a few words to say as well.'

Mrs. Lovell laid a restraining hand on her husband's arm. Finny felt it was probably Mrs. Lovell's job in life to hold Martin back, and it was a tribute to one or the other, that he always seemed to listen to her.

The identity of the pills had apparently been established, Miss Lovell being a patient of Dr. O'Brien's. Finny mentioned the quantity of drink. 'How is she?' he asked the doctor.

'We'll have to see how the treatment works,' responded the medical man cheerfully, and feeling his heart's desire was in good hands, Finny returned to tackle her parents.

Martin met him with sincere apologies. 'My wife has just told me,' he began, 'how you brought Geraldine home and looked after her. We're very grateful.'

In the end they all went and sat on an uncomfortable bench in the corridor, and some time later, in the early hours of the morning, a member of the staff approached with the news that Geraldine was 'responding'.

7

This day, which was to spread the name of Gifford to places where it was hitherto unknown, began for its townspeople as most other days.

Early in the morning, church bells could be heard. The Gifford fishermen had already put out to sea. Small shopkeepers opened their doors for newspaper sales. Milk roundsmen appeared on the streets. Early commuters queued for the bus to take them to the railway station, situated as these stations occasionally are, remote from human habitation. Thus Gifford railway station also served the village of Rathnowl.

Over at Furry Park House, the Lovells had returned from the hospital, their night's vigil ending with the medical verdict on their daughter's condition as being 'satisfactory'. She would be in hospital for a day or so. Husband and wife surveyed one another pensively across the breakfast table, and Martin said: 'When Geraldine comes home, we've got to get at the root of this trouble.'

His wife looked at him anxiously: 'It's only natural she should be upset and out of sorts. Look what she's been through. I blame the doctor for not having told her about drinking.'

'The poor man probably had no idea she drank. Grace, we've got to make that girl tell us what has made her this way. She could have killed herself.'

'If it hadn't been for Mr. Raftery, you mean.'

'Yes, and that's another thing. That fellow was very conveniently on the scene, don't you think?'

'He's a young man, Martin. He has time off. Why shouldn't he go to a dance?'

'Here, in the town!'

'Why not? And he spoke very nicely to me last night and to you, in spite of your rudeness. I think he's taken a fancy to our Geraldine.'

Martin opened his mouth to reply, and

then changed his mind. In view of this latest occurrence, he'd have to see Brennan again. On the last occasion, following the abortive interview with Raftery, when the real solicitor, Brennan, had arrived and Martin had outlined the situation to him, the legal man had advised a 'wait and see' policy, and had accepted Miss Lovell's almost hysterical refusal to let him near her with a philosophical rejoinder that 'in the circumstances it might be for the best.' This last remark had upset Martin more than he cared to admit.

'Going to make a few phone calls,' he said now, getting up from the table and moving towards the door.

Grace was reminded of some letters she had intended writing. 'I must get some stamps, while I'm at the shops today,' she said.

Their daughter, who had spent a very unpleasant night and was still suffering from its after effects, was cheered by the arrival of a spectacular bouquet of pink and yellow roses; Finny being sensitive enough not to send red flowers to a girl with that shade of hair.

Her recollections of the previous evening were hazy in the extreme, but perversely, the scene which her memory retained was the one in which basin and towel had figured largely. The extravagant flowers bore witness to at least one fact, that Detective Raftery's interest had survived his ordeal of the night before, and as she lay on her narrow hospital bed, Geraldine came to regard him in quite a favourable light.

Meanwhile, still ignorant of these events, Inspector Coen was pursuing routine enquiries which necessitated his return to the city. A television appeal for information had netted one gentleman who positively identified Simon Connolly as having shared a cabin with him on the Holyhead — Dublin night sailing of March 8th. According to this witness, a meticulous and opinionated fellow, Simon had been taciturn and his manner secretive not to say peculiar. Subjected to the machine gun prattle of his informant, Moss, who longed to place as great a distance as possible between himself and it, noted this peculiarity with a query.

The blanket bore the label of a well-known Dublin store, and was tentatively identified by a member of the sales staff as having been sold possibly early in March, and almost certainly to a woman customer. Suspecting this was fairly hopeless anyway, Moss ventured to enquire if the buyer might have been a tall red- or fair-haired girl, very attractive in appearance, to which the answer appeared to be that no one could remember such a person having bought a blanket in the recent past. A more settled person, most likely.

After an exhausting round of engravers and die-sinkers, the Inspector located one Edward Poddle, the elderly sole survivor of a long-established engraving firm in Bridgefoot Street. Mr. Poddle's records were designed to facilitate a one-man operation and were therefore easy of access. The plate was his workmanship. Ordered by phone, it had been collected by a man who paid cash. No, unhappily Mr. Poddle's memory wasn't as good as it had been. He couldn't remember what the fellow looked like. April 14th was the date. Oh no, it couldn't have been a woman. There hadn't been a woman in Mr. Poddle's shop since . . . here Mr. Poddle lost himself in distant realms.

The button and the earring still remained. The former was a wash-out of course. Half the male population must be wearing similar ones. The earring was a slightly better proposition. Pierced ears could be noted. Geraldine Lovell's ears were pierced. Not that this meant anything. The earring could have been dropped there at any time, and these days men as well as women had pierced ears. The envelope addressed to Rita Mulholland had yielded nothing.

And so away to Gifford and in the afternoon a conference with Finny, Tom O'Shea and Noonan in attendance.

The proceedings opened with a detailed report from Sergeant O'Shea on enquiries made into the whereabouts of Lily Sullivan, no letter having as yet been received from that source. Next, Detective Raftery gave a carefully edited description of his encounter with Miss

Lovell, a recital to some extent capped by the Inspector's own experiences with the same lady. Moss then went on to summarise the results of his investigations, and in so doing, he produced further notes which he had made.

'Out of all this,' he said, 'the first and most important fact we have discovered,' this with a smile in Tom's direction, 'is that Lily Sullivan is apparently alive and being sheltered by her family. There is a good chance she may be able to tell us a lot we want to know, and since it seems certain she has returned to this country, we ought to be able to trace her without too much bother. And we have some other facts; for instance, the date on which Connolly returned to Dublin — the morning of March 8th. Can we learn anything from that?'

'He was here for two or three days before he was killed,' Finny said, 'always supposing the plate gave the true date of death. There were no prints on the plate, were there?'

'No,' replied Moss shortly, 'shouldn't expect to get any, when it had been pushed into the ground. For the moment, we'll accept March 11th as the day he died. Now the engraver of the brass plate, Mr. Poddle, is certain no woman called to his premises, and that the plate was ordered, collected and paid for by a man. On the other hand, the blanket is believed to have been purchased by a woman. So here we have the set-up which I suggested at the outset; a man and a woman working together. Unfortunately for my earlier theory, the woman apparently bears no resemblance to Geraldine Lovell.'

Finny, who seemed to swallow too hastily, was overcome by a fit of coughing and Sergeant O'Shea regarded him with a good deal of sympathy.

Moss went on as though there had been no interruption: 'Both witnesses have promised to contact us immediately if they should either of them remember anything else relevant. Now the woman is described as being 'settled'. Any ideas on that?'

Tom said, rather unhappily they all thought: 'There's Mary Purcell of course.'

'Where's the motive?'

'Would she protect the Connolly family from some kind of scandal?' asked Finny, eager to explore motives for anyone other than his inamorata.

'To the extent of secretly burying a corpse?' Moss sounded incredulous.

When put into words, it did sound far-fetched. Yet they afterwards realised that those few remarks, correctly interpreted, might have solved the case, and with none of the agony still to come. As it was, the enquiry team abandoned this line, and went on to Moss's next point, namely, that Lily Sullivan was not the only one who could tell them about Simon Connolly's last days.

'Miss Lovell almost certainly knows what happened to him, and why,' Moss said grimly.

'Ye don't know that,' Tom cut in, 'it's only guesswork.'

'It's more than that now. Anyhow, interrogation while she's in hospital is just not on, with all the fuss it would stir up, but as soon as she's discharged, I'm going to get her down here for questioning,

Martin Lovell or no Martin Lovell.'

He finished with a glare at O'Shea and a sideways glance at Finny, who was gazing out of the window.

'Raftery, could you spare us your kind attention for a moment. Is Miss Lovell friendly towards you?'

O'Shea gave a muffled guffaw, and Moss shot him a dark look.

'Right, well as long as she doesn't chuck things at you! I want you to get back to the hospital and sit with the patient this evening. Stay there until they throw you out, you understand. No matter what parents, relatives or friends come and go, you are to stay until she's tucked up for the night. And Noonan — we'll put you on duty there tomorrow, O.K?'

'Yes, sir,' replied Noonan, much gratified.

Finny made no reply, but he was already reaching for his jacket.

Moss said warningly: 'Remember, I don't want to wake up tomorrow and find Miss Lovell recuperating in the Bahamas or whatever other distant spot Daddy's money will pay for. If there's anything you can't cope with, buzz us quick and we'll send help, right?'

But the urgent call, when it did come, was not from that source. Finny had been gone an hour and two extra men who were on relief duty were preparing to leave for the day, when Noonan, in the outer office, took the call.

Sheila Curran suddenly burst into the inner room. 'Moss!' she cried.

'What is it, girl?' asked O'Shea, but Moss pushed past him and went out to Noonan.

The latter was writing on a pad, and as he listened he put his hand over the mouthpiece for a second.

'Ring the hospital, sir,' he said urgently, 'a shooting at Coltsfoot Lane — lady says there's three shot and they think one of them's dead.'

Moss was already dialling the hospital number. After he got through, he said rapidly to Noonan: 'Get all the details you can, and then get ready to come with me. Tom . . . ' he looked round, but Tom and the two relief men were already piling into the car outside.

He put down the phone. 'Sheila,' he said, 'we'll have to leave you to hold things here for a while. Get on to H.Q. and pass them the report. We'll need reinforcements. Oh, and ring the exchange. Have them hold open the lines to the post office. If the lines are down . . . '

'O.K., O.K. I know the drill.'

The Inspector left without another word.

8

Coltsfoot Lane, that pleasant relic of more leisurely days, presented a scene unparalleled in its history when Moss and Noonan reached it.

A narrow thoroughfare in normal times, it was now effectively blocked at both ends by the large crowd which had gathered. Sergeant O'Shea's car, penetrating some way into the throng, had been halted, and the Sergeant having left it, his voice could be heard imploring people to 'stand back there' an impossible procedure for them to adopt, as their retreat first necessitated the evacuation of persons on the fringe of the crowd, and even as he spoke, fresh numbers arrived and crowded in.

Moss, who was driving, handed over to Noonan and got out, forcing the door open against numbers of people, and none too gently.

'Let me pass there,' he said tersely, and

elbowed his way forward, shoving and digging with his elbows.

On the footpath, outside the post office, a man lay moaning. He held his left thigh, while a woman knelt on the ground beside him and endeavoured to improvise a tourniquet. He had lost a fair amount of blood.

Moss entered the shop, carefully stepping over another prone figure. He stooped and felt the man's pulse, which was still. Outside, an ambulance siren could be heard coming up the street.

Lying on the coconut matting and being attended by three women and a man, was the owner of the shop, Mary Purcell. Her face was very white and her eyes were closed.

One of the women looked up as Moss came in. 'Are you the doctor?' she asked.

'The ambulance is here now,' he replied gently.

The man at the back of the group came over to Moss. 'She's hurt bad,' he said, 'get her away as fast as you can.'

A second and third ambulance could be heard screaming their way towards them. The first stretcher party seemed inclined to halt beside the man with the leg wound, and Moss went out and brought them in to where Miss Purcell lay. From behind the counter came other sounds of distress and the Inspector went to investigate.

The young girl with the dark glasses, Mary Purcell's assistant, sat huddled on the floor rocking to and fro. She seemed to shrink away as Moss came near, and he bent down and spoke to her, as though soothing a frightened animal. 'Are you hurt, miss?'

She did not answer and gave no sign of recognition. He went outside and commandeered an ambulance driver.

'There's a girl behind the shop counter,' he said to the man, 'a bad case of shock I think.'

The man passed his hand across his forehead.

'It's like a bloody massacre,' he said. 'What happened, do you think?'

'We'll find out,' said Moss, 'better get that girl away.'

As the men carried out the last

stretcher, two more squad cars and another car screeched their way into Coltsfoot Lane. The men got out, and the door of the third car opened to reveal a member of the local clergy. He looked a little helplessly at the three ambulances, the first of which was about to pull away. The door of the second was just closing and the priest sprinted forward and got in at the last moment.

Sergeant O'Shea, who had been speaking into his car telephone, came over to Moss.

'Headquarters wants a word with you, sir.'

'Coen here,' said Moss, taking the instrument from him.

When the Sergeant rejoined him, it was to find his superior for once rather at a loss. 'Did you get orders, sir?' the Sergeant enquired.

Moss looked speculatively at him. 'What did you tell them?'

'I said, sir, that Mary Purcell was a key witness in your case, and now she'd been shot and may die, poor soul.'

'Miss Purcell a key witness?'

'About Lily Sullivan,' the Sergeant said reproachfully, 'I thought it only right to make that point.'

'The point being,' Moss exploded, 'that the station sergeant in Gifford doesn't want a second criminal investigation team prosecuting enquiries in this area, and tripping over himself and his men in the process.'

'Ye could put it like that,' O'Shea replied with a grin. 'Sure we haven't the room anyhow. Did they ask you to take the job, sir?'

'Of course they did,' Moss snapped, 'and stop saying 'sir'.'

'One thing anyhow,' the Sergeant went on, 'we'll get plenty of reinforcements now.'

Another car pulled in to dislodge the fingerprint boys and their gear, and Moss put them to work immediately, leaving the post office and its environs to their functions. Across the street, ten or twelve witnesses had been collected and names and addresses were being taken.

Moss buttonholed the Sergeant. 'Keep them all together till you've finished with them,' he said. 'By the way, who's that fellow hovering round the post office?'

'Fergus Doyle of the *Gifford & Rathnowl Weekly*,' replied the Sergeant promptly.

'Oh Lord, I suppose we'll have the Dublin bunch on top of us soon.'

'And a TV crew.'

'Right, well your witnesses are geese for the plucking, so get going before you lose any.'

Moss crossed the road, keeping an eye on the wily Fergus. However, here a diversion occurred, and a member of the police team working inside the post office emerged hurriedly and made straight for the Inspector. He paused as he noticed Mr. Doyle, and the significance of the pause was not lost on Moss or on the newspaper man. With an upraised hand Moss warded off the latter's unspoken questions, and dashed into the post office with the policeman at his heels. The Garda on duty smartly closed the door behind them, leaving a frustrated Mr. Doyle outside.

Once inside the shop, the reason for the

urgent call became apparent. In the centre of the floor a woman sat on one of Mary Purcell's better chairs, apparently brought from the inner room. She was of middle age, slight, fair-haired, and was sipping a glass of water.

The man who had fetched Moss said at once: 'We didn't see her at first, but she was here all the time.'

The woman looked up. 'Are you the Inspector?' she asked.

'I'm Inspector Coen, yes.'

She put aside the glass of water and held out her hand. 'I've heard a great deal about you from my daughter, whom I believe you know. I'm Grace Lovell, Geraldine's mother.'

Rather mechanically he shook hands with her. He could not figure her position here, and she seemed to sense his perplexity, for she said at once: 'I came in to buy some stamps. I was on my way home and had forgotten to get some earlier.'

'Can you tell us what happened?' he asked abruptly.

'Well, I can tell you what happened at

the beginning; afterwards, I fainted I think.'

'Where was she found?' Moss queried one of the men.

'In a cupboard,' the man said, and Mrs. Lovell cut in at once.

'Oh I know it must seem stupid,' she said, 'but I'll tell you just how it came about.'

Moss intervened. 'I'll run you home first,' he said. 'No,' he went on as she protested, 'you should have gone to the hospital, really.'

'Well I'm certainly not going to any hospital,' replied Grace Lovell with a glint in her eyes. 'One member of the family in hospital is quite enough.'

'O.K.,' Moss said easily, 'come along now, and you can tell me all about it as we go.'

However, by the time he had outmanoeuvred Mr. Doyle, collected his car and assisted Mrs. Lovell into it, he had decided to postpone his questioning until they should have reached her home. Here they were greeted by an anxious Martin Lovell, who, seeing his wife helped out of a police car, hurriedly emerged from the house to meet them.

'Now Martin,' said his wife, 'there's nothing the matter with me a cup of tea wouldn't put right, so get me one please and the Inspector and I will sit and talk in the drawing-room.'

'Where's Geraldine?' he asked sharply.

'Still at the hospital, I expect. At least I haven't seen her anyway. This afternoon's events have quite taken my mind off our daughter.'

Her husband looked from one to the other, and then said rather surprisingly: 'I'll tell Bridget to get you some tea.'

Mrs. Lovell removed her light summer coat and sat close to the coal fire which burned low in the grate. Martin came in almost immediately, and demanded: 'Now tell me Grace, just what is going on around here?'

'To begin with, Martin,' she replied, slightly enjoying herself, 'I was in the post office this afternoon when it was held up by two men. I had gone in to buy some stamps and Miss Purcell's assistant was serving me, when the door burst open and a man came into the shop, holding a gun in his hand. He said for us to stand away from the counter.'

Martin came over and sat down beside her. 'My dear,' he said, in a voice quite unlike his usual one, 'you weren't hurt at all, were you?'

She looked at him and smiled. 'Not in the least,' she said. 'I just fainted, but that was later.'

'So long as you're all right,' he said, and squeezed her shoulders. 'Oh here's Bridget,' and he went to take a tray from the housekeeper, who had put out three cups.

'You'll have a cup with us, Inspector?' he said quite politely, and Moss reflected humorously that his wife must have worked on him persistently to have achieved this result. When they had all been served with tea and some ham sandwiches, Mrs. Lovell continued with her narrative.

In response to a question from the Inspector as to whether she could identify the man with the gun, she said: 'He was stocky, about twenty-eight or so, with straight black hair, badly cut,' this description fitting the man found dead inside the door.

'After you moved away from the counter, what did he do next?'

'He told Mary Purcell's assistant — Deidre I think her name is — to put all the money on the counter and also he was talking about Social Insurance stamps, but she just stood there and looked frozen, if you know what I mean. Then he began shouting at her, saying he would kill her if she didn't do as he said, and with that, the door at the back of the shop opened and Miss Purcell herself looked out — she heard all the noise I suppose. She slammed the door again very quickly, and you could hear the key turn in the lock.'

Martin Lovell laughed shortly: 'That must have upset the fellow's plans, I'd say. What did he do then?'

About to ask the same question, Moss writing busily, devoutly hoped Mrs. Lovell's faint hadn't occurred at this crucial moment. However, she went on steadily:

'I suppose I should have guessed the man wouldn't be on his own,' she said. 'Anyhow, when Mary Purcell locked herself into the back room, he moved over to the street door, covering us with the gun all the time. Then he came back inside, and another man came in with him but remained standing at the door.'

'Did he have a gun too?' queried Moss.

'He could have had. I didn't actually see it though, because I was afraid to turn round.'

'And he just stood at the door?'

'That's right. The first man came right over to the counter again. I think he knew Deidre wasn't going to be any good to him. Her face was very pale and she was just staring the whole time. Then he shot the lock off the inner door.'

'That was the first shot?'

'Yes. It frightened me terribly, and it must have been the end for poor Deidre. When I looked again, she had disappeared — presumably she just slipped down behind the counter.'

'That's where we found her,' Moss said. 'What about you?'

'Oh, I was still all right at that stage. With the lock shattered, the man then kicked in the door and shouted to Miss Purcell to come out.'

'He called her by name?'

'Yes.'

'Could he actually see her?'

'I don't think so, in fact I'm sure he couldn't.' Mrs. Lovell swallowed some tea, and then went on: 'She must have been standing parallel with him, on the other side of the wall. Then there were two more shots, louder than the first.'

'Was anyone hit?'

'The man at the door to the street. He gave a terrible cry and, when I looked, he had gone. Is he dead?'

Martin looked from one to the other in a kind of horror, but Moss said evenly enough: 'If it was the man we found outside, then no. He has a bad thigh wound, but as far as we know he'll be all right.'

Martin turned to his wife and said, incredulously: 'Miss Purcell shot him?'

She patted his hand. 'I think she did, dear.'

'And what did you do while this was going on?'

'Well,' she said, 'I decided I was quite likely to be killed if I stayed where I was. The man with the gun had turned his back to me, and I was almost directly behind him, and behind me, all the glass shelving! I envied poor Deidre, probably unconscious, and certainly out of the line of fire in her snug corner. So I looked round quickly and I saw this press in the wall at the end of the knitting counter. I didn't actually expect to be able to get into it, but I felt if I held the door open, it would give me some protection. The door looked very solid.

'After edging my way slowly backwards I had almost reached it when the man turned round and saw me. Then for an instant, I saw Mary Purcell in the inner doorway. She had him covered with her shotgun. She said 'drop the gun or I'll shoot,' or something to that effect. My legs felt very weak. Suddenly I didn't care any more. I reached back, found the knob of the cupboard door, pulled it open, and then everything went a bit hazy.

'I heard the man moving, and then there were two more shots and a sound like a chair falling over, and I remember screaming, and pulling at the door as hard as I could. After that, the next thing I remember is seeing a chink of light where the cupboard door was slightly ajar, and hearing people moving about outside, and wondering where I was and what had happened to me.'

Martin Lovell put his arms round his wife and kissed her. 'Darling,' he said, 'you're going to be able to dine out on this story for the rest of your life. I wish I had as good a tale to tell.' But his voice, when he spoke, was anything but normal.

Grace said: 'What happened to Mary Purcell; is she all right?'

'I'm afraid not,' Moss replied. 'She was shot twice in the chest. She's alive, but for how long we don't know.'

'Good God,' Martin said. 'How did she come to have a gun?'

'Oh, I know about that dear. It belonged to her grandfather, I think. My father knew the old man you know, and he said he always kept a gun on the premises. I expect it's the same one. Anyhow she had it in the back room always. It was in a long stool, with a red plush covered seat.'

'How many people knew it was there?' queried Moss, at the same time wishing this information was coming from another source. Mrs. Lovell's proving so helpful was an irony, when her daughter might be wanted by the police in another case, or perhaps in the same case.

Grace appeared to believe that the whereabouts of the gun was known to most of the older residents. At this point the phone in the hall rang and Martin excused himself and went to answer it. He was gone a few minutes and then came back saying the Inspector was wanted. Moss left the room.

Grace looked up, and Martin nodded meaningly. 'Detective Raftery!' he said. 'Sounded in a bit of a stew,' he added, 'seems he tried several numbers before he finally caught up with his boss. What do you think of Coen, by the way?'

'He is rather abrupt, I suppose,' his wife passed a limp hand across her forehead.

'Martin, we should ring Geraldine. She's bound to hear of this — particularly being in the same hospital. She'll be very upset.'

'Oh, I imagine young Finnbarr will tell her.'

'Finnbarr?'

'Yes,' her husband grinned wickedly, 'Detective Raftery's name is Finnbarr. Didn't you know?'

'What has he got to do with it?'

'He was telephoning from the hospital just now.'

'I expect he would be far too concerned about the man who was wounded, and of course poor Mary Purcell.'

Martin, whose brief conversation with Finny had given him quite a different impression, was on the point of saying so, when the Inspector having finished his call, returned to them, saying he must be off.

'I'll call again tomorrow,' Moss added briefly. He was thinking of the necessary identification of the man at the hospital.

Before the bad news broke, Finny and

Geraldine had spent a very pleasant couple of hours. To begin with, the sight of his flowers tastefully arranged and displayed in a prominent position beside the bed, heartened him.

Miss Lovell, in a soft and pliant mood, chatted agreeably on a variety of subjects. Although not too experienced in these matters, even Finny was aware of her efforts to please him. It seemed she was interested in his home, his family. Naturally, he endeavoured to ask a few questions also, but she was not very forthcoming. Predictably, it turned out she played a good deal of tennis during the summer months, and also some golf. Then there was sailing of course.

The room was a private one, and the only recurring interruptions were the half-hourly visits from one or other of the nurses who knew who Raftery was, if not exactly his reason for being there. However, his long stay inevitably begged the question, if only from the patient herself.

When she asked it, she reached out and took hold of his arm, looking straight up into his face. 'Finny,' she said, 'why did you come — I mean, really why?'

He wasn't much good at light badinage, but he prayed he might keep nimblc just for this one. How long he could hope to make things last, was another thing.

'I'm just crazy about you,' he said, and laughed. Then he looked away.

'Crazy?' she said, but there was a soft catch in her voice.

The room was empty and no amount of professional etiquette was going to hold him now. She was half inclined to him anyway, and when he sat up on the bed she came into his arms as if the memory of being there the previous night were fresh in her mind. When he had seen her at the inquest five days before, he could not have imagined such a scene. She hardly waited for him to kiss her, but put her arms round him in a practised way.

When she let him go, she allowed him to lower her gently onto the pillows. He still sat on the bed, with his hands on her shoulders.

'I love you, Gerry,' he said, and then

stroked wisps of hair away from her face.

'Do you?' she asked wonderingly. 'It hasn't been very long.'

'Long enough.'

'You don't know me. I mean, we've only met twice, not counting the times we didn't speak.'

'You saw me at the inquest?'

She smiled, and the hardness went out of her face. 'Sure, and then you came to the house. I heard Mum and Dad had their solicitor locked up with them. I saw you leave and knew who you were. Then I bawled them out for being such idiots.' She caught hold of his sleeve and said playfully: 'My mother likes you, Finnbarr Raftery. Did you know that?'

He flushed. 'She's terribly nice,' he said.

'Yes, she is.' There was a wistfulness in her voice. Then she said suddenly and violently: 'Why did you have to be in the police? Mum and I can't talk. There are things . . . '

He didn't know how to answer. Dying to get at the truth, yet afraid of what she might say, he reflected that it couldn't be very bad. But her attitude worried him.

'I'm not a policeman all the time,' he managed at last, but when he looked at her, he knew the moment had gone.

A silence fell. He was trying to nerve himself to say what he had wanted to say from the beginning. He took a deep breath: 'I want you to marry me.'

What her reply might have been he could not guess. He saw her expression alter, but at that moment the door burst open and a distracted nurse grabbed hold of Finny, sliding on the highly polished floor.

'There's been a shooting in the town,' she gasped. 'The ambulances are coming in. They want you down in the front office.'

Finny jumped up, but all the same he remembered his commission from Moss. 'I'll be down directly,' he said to the nurse. 'Tell them I'm coming.'

Geraldine exclaimed: 'A shooting in Gifford!' The nurse went out and shut the door.

'It may be a bank raid — someone hurt,' Finny said, coming over to the bed.

He took her hand. 'Listen to me. I want you to promise me no matter what happens you'll stay here till I get back. A real promise, you understand?'

She looked up at him and gave his hand a squeeze. 'I promise,' she said. 'Kiss me again.'

When he came away, he felt he had reason to be very pleased with his afternoon's work.

9

By eleven o'clock the following morning, a great deal had happened, and the case or both cases, had begun to snowball.

Moss had risen early, read the morning newspapers, with the previous day's events set forth in banner headlines together with a photograph of Mary Purcell, apparently taken at somebody's wedding. The Superintendent had arrived, been interviewed by the press, promised early arrests, and had visited the hospital.

Mrs. Lovell had been collected from her home, taken to the hospital, and in the presence of the police on duty there had identified the dead man and the man with the leg wound as the two who had held up the post office. The man with the leg wound, now recovering from an operation and stated to be 'comfortable' although weak from loss of blood and post-operative shock, refused to answer questions.

In the hospital's intensive care unit, Mary Purcell still clung to life. In two operations, it had proved impossible to remove the second bullet. Shrouded in masks and gowns, Moss and the Superintendent had been admitted to see her. The unit, lit by three long heavily-curtained windows and staffed by four nurses, was under the direction of a senior staff sister. Even the Superintendent looked apologetic as he and Moss tiptoed over to the bed and peered anxiously at its occupant.

Her face had a greenish hue and her breathing was laboured. An oxygen tube was fixed to one nostril, and the bed seemed to be covered with other tubes trailing to various items of apparatus standing or hanging by the bed. Her eyes were closed. Tiptoeing out of the room, and divesting themselves of the surgical gowns, the two men went to interview the surgeon and his assistant.

The medical verdict, delivered with many qualifications, was that Mary Purcell's internal haemorrhaging might cease or, alternatively, become worse.

That in the operations already performed, they had failed to stop the bleeding or remove the second bullet. That a third operation, while giving no greater hope of success, was likely to prove fatal. Even to tough police ears, this did not sound encouraging.

The gun which Mary Purcell had used, had been recovered and held for evidence, likewise the two guns found with the raiders. Deidre Hogan, the sixteen-year-old post office clerk, was still suffering from shock, and although interviewed by the police, was unable to make a statement or indeed to offer any coherent account of the previous day's events.

There remained therefore the evidence of Mrs. Lovell. This good lady was now sitting with her daughter, another thorn in the side of Inspector Coen. Mrs. Lovell was being very co-operative indeed, but for how long would she remain so if he interrogated Geraldine as he had threatened to do. Also, although Finny Raftery had come back on duty at the hospital like a homing pigeon, he couldn't afford to keep him there. In fact, much as he disliked to admit it, he needed Raftery for other work.

Accordingly, Finny, standing patiently outside the ward door and waiting for Geraldine's mother to depart, was eventually told by Moss that 'he could leave off that now.'

The patient looked wan and had slept hardly at all, and naturally her mother attributed these pale looks to the recent ordeals suffered by both.

'I'm quite all right, Gerry,' she said reassuringly, 'not so much as a scratch or a bump. Now you are not to worry at all, and the doctor says we can have you home later in the day.'

'Sure Mum. You were terribly lucky nothing serious happened to you. Mary Purcell is in a very bad way, I believe.'

A spasm of anxiety crossed Mrs. Lovell's face. 'Poor soul,' she said, 'she never meant to let them get the money. She must have known the danger. And then there's poor Deidre as well.'

'Deidre?'

'Oh, you know the girl who came to

replace Lily — a dark-haired girl with large spectacles.'

'No,' said Geraldine flatly, 'I don't believe I've been in that place since Lily left it.'

Mrs. Lovell looked at her daughter with some concern. 'My dear, you're not still brooding about Simon are you? If I were you, I'd put the whole thing out of my mind once and for all.'

Geraldine said nothing and just turned away her head.

'What about this Deidre?' she asked, after a pause.

The silence had been so oppressive, her mother was glad to fall back on this subject.

'My dear, she's had a very bad shock indeed. The doctor thinks it's partly her age, but apparently she's always been more than just timid and shy, rather 'withdrawn' in fact. I met her mother when I went in to see the girl. A very nice woman, I must say, and nearly going out of her mind with worry. The girl probably takes after her. Anyhow, she poured the whole thing out to me. Glad to have someone to talk it over with, I expect.'

Geraldine smiled almost in spite of herself. This was so typical of her mother. When she saw her daughter's smile, Mrs. Lovell cheered up.

'You'll feel better once you're away from this place,' she said, looking distastefully at the pale green walls and dark green floor. Her attention focused on the floral decorations. 'What beautiful roses!' she exclaimed. 'Who sent them?'

'My detective friend. They arrived yesterday morning.'

Mrs. Lovell sat up, vindicated. 'There now,' she said, 'I knew there was something in it.' Her feminine instincts aroused, she leant forward eagerly: 'What do you think of him, dear?'

Geraldine glanced sideways at her mother. 'You like him, don't you?'

Grace Lovell smiled and sat back in her chair. 'I took a fancy to that boy the first time we met. Even your father doesn't dislike him now. Only last night, he said to me he thought Finny was a 'good enough' fellow, and of course . . . '

' . . . his father is the Judge,' Geraldine's voice was hard.

'There's nothing the matter with the legal profession,' her mother answered with some asperity, 'and when I think of the families of the boyfriends you've had in the past — of, what was that fellow's name . . . Brian, wasn't it? Martin said his people were smooth operators, downright crooks, in fact.'

Her daughter sighed. 'There was never anything serious with Brian. He was fun to be with, that's all.'

'And not that I care to speak ill of the dead . . . '

Geraldine gave a cry, almost of anguish. 'Oh God, no Mum, leave that be.'

Mrs. Lovell subsided, and there was silence for a moment. Then she continued in more normal tones: 'Finny Raftery seems very attentive.'

Geraldine said baldly: 'He's asked me to marry him.'

She had the satisfaction of watching her mother's start of surprise. 'You can't be serious! It's been only a few days.'

'I know. I told him that. He seems very sure. I told him he couldn't know anything about me.'

A calculating look came into her mother's eyes. 'You haven't refused him, have you?' she enquired anxiously.

'I didn't get the chance. I told him I wished he hadn't been a detective.'

Her mother seized on this objection in a practical way. 'He's very young still,' she said, 'plenty of time for him to switch to something more suitable.' Her mind flitted over a series of mental pictures, commencing with her future son-in-law being called to the Bar, and ending with her being present at his inauguration as President of the High Court.

Geraldine looked at her mother in affectionate understanding. 'I keep forgetting,' she said, 'that you've been through a bad time yesterday. Sorry I'm a bit snappish. Just at the moment I can hardly even bear to think about Finny.'

Mrs. Lovell was all contrition. 'My dear, I'm perfectly all right. You're the patient. Now I must go anyway. Martin is coming to collect you this evening, and if

Finny is off duty and here at the hospital, be sure and invite him for tea. I'm warning you,' she added playfully, 'if you turn him down, I'll divorce your father and marry him myself.'

Geraldine laughed at that, but when her mother was gone her expression changed and she looked very serious indeed.

'I've got to decide what to do now,' she brooded to herself, 'and there's only one person I can talk to.' She got out of bed and went to make a phone call.

When Moss came back to the station, O'Shea was full of questions. 'Did ye get an identification of the dead man?'

'We know he was the man who shot Mary Purcell, but we still don't know who he is.'

'What about the other fellow?'

'So far he's refused to identify his companion, even though the doctors told him the man was dead. I don't think he believed them. At first he refused to say anything at all, but finally he gave his own name as Noel Deane, aged twenty-two, with a Dublin city address. It's being checked out now. If we can get any relatives to come forward, we can clear up that matter straight away. And we are circulating a description of the dead man. People are usually willing enough to identify once the fellow's dead.'

'That's the way of it,' agreed Sergeant O'Shea, with a sigh.

Meanwhile, Detective Raftery was pursuing enquiries likely to keep him occupied for some days to come. The Inspector felt it was necessary to compile a dossier on each of the persons in any way connected with Simon Connolly, and for this purpose Finny had been dispatched to the offices of the Custom House to enquire into the family records of the Sullivans, Connollys etc. and of course, most important of all, the Lovell family. Even Turlough McClintock had not been omitted, for a remark made by him when at the funeral had raised a query in the Inspector's mind.

Following Moss's instructions and his own inclination, Finny commenced work by researching into the Lovell menage. Geraldine's birth certificate, easily found, yielded the surname of Mrs. Lovell's autocratic father, and from Grace's own certificate, he emerged in full. So that was who he was, mused his prospective grandson-in-law. Well, any opposition emanating from his own domestic circle should be stifled in part at least by the revelation of the great man's name. He laughed to himself as he remembered Grace's description of her father's reception of Martin Lovell as his daughter's choice; in the circumstances quite understandable.

Later, returning to his own home front, he remembered he had arranged to play a round of golf with his father that evening, and felt it might be no bad idea to break the news of possible impending nuptials. Probably fortunately for his father's enjoyment of the game, when Finny arrived at the clubhouse, he discovered that a foursome had been arranged.

Finny played disappointing golf, his concentration being poor, and when they were on the way home, having concluded the evening with a few drinks, the Judge said: 'You look done-in Finny; is this case likely to go on much longer?'

'I'm afraid it will — a while longer anyway, but it's not that, it's something else. I wanted to tell you earlier this evening, but we didn't get any time to ourselves.'

'Sounds a bit serious. You are not in any kind of trouble, are you?'

Finny, who was driving, gave a quick shake of the head and then grinned. 'I suppose you could say I was — and the worst kind too.'

The Judge turned and regarded his son for a moment. 'You don't sound particularly worried by it.'

Finny laughed a bit incoherently, and Mr. Raftery, senior, gave a slow nod reminiscent of his days in the courtroom, and a smile born of experience then illuminated his face, which was quite a pleasant one.

'Ah,' he said, 'an affair of the heart perhaps?'

'I've asked her to marry me,' said Finny, thinking it better to come straight out with it.

'And has she accepted you?'

'Not yet.'

'Not a woman to rush into anything?'

'I don't know. She's impulsive enough in some ways.'

The Judge said patiently: 'Obviously, you'll want to tell me all about her. Park the car outside the house, and we'll have a natter.' He looked out of the window and added, a little self-consciously: 'Your mother will still be up, I expect.'

'Ma will just love her,' Finny said, 'and Charlie too.'

The elder Mr. Raftery gave a discreet chuckle. 'Oh, I can quite see how Charlie's acceptance of a sister-in-law is a matter upon which the peace of the whole household will depend. Well, are you going to tell me who she is?'

This was the invitation to Finny to display his recently acquired knowledge and he said at once: 'She is the grand-daughter of someone you used to know in the old days,' and he named the man.

'Really? Good Lord. Well, I knew he had a daughter of course. In fact I met her on several occasions. A very pretty little thing, and his only child I think.

Whom did she marry?'

'She is married to Martin Lovell,' replied his son, without finesse.

The elder man settled back into his seat, and stretched his legs as if to ease a cramp. When he spoke, it was in an altered tone.

'What you are telling me is this; you want to marry Geraldine Lovell, the girl who is mixed up in the Connolly case. How long have you known her?'

'Five days.'

'You can't possibly get to know anyone in five days.'

'That's just what she says. But the first day I saw her I felt I knew her quite well. I can't describe it. I hadn't even spoken to her.'

'When was this; at the inquest?'

'Yes.'

His father digested this in silence and then said at last: 'So, she's the old man's granddaughter. You were right to tell me that.' He paused, 'Are you saying you love her, really love her I mean?'

Finny swallowed, and looked away. 'Yes,' he said.

'And does she love you?'

'She hasn't said so.'

His father smiled. 'My dear Finnbarr, your reply would do credit to a member of my profession.'

Finny said awkwardly: 'She seems to care for me, a bit.'

'I should very much like to meet her, or is that possible just at present?'

'She's in hospital, at the moment.'

His father was genuinely concerned. 'Nothing serious I hope?'

'It could have been, but it turned out O.K. She's worried stiff over this case.'

The elder man became quite sympathetic. 'Poor child,' he said, 'her evidence at the inquest was very courageously given, I thought.'

Finny warmed to him. 'She was absolutely splendid,' he said.

'You won't take this amiss, will you,' his father went on, 'does she have a good solicitor?'

Finny managed a laugh. Then he said: 'They have Brennan I believe — Flannan Brennan, that is.'

The Judge nodded approvingly. 'Very

sound, very sound indeed . . . ' he broke off, 'and your position in all this — it must be rather difficult?'

'Sheer hell,' replied his son matter-of-factly.

His father permitted himself a smile, but his eyes looked grave. 'You're still working for Inspector Coen, are you?'

'Oh yes, and he's on this other case as well.'

'Which case?'

'The post office raid. The one where the sub-postmistress was shot and another man killed.'

'You'll take care of yourself, Finny, will you not? I don't have to tell you . . . '

'Oh sure,' Finny replied offhandedly, 'I don't aim to get myself killed. Anyhow, that part of it is all over. As a matter of fact I was at the hospital with Geraldine when it happened.'

His father did not lose his worried look. 'Is Inspector Coen aware of your . . . interest . . . in Miss Lovell?'

Finny nodded. 'I think he's got wind of something all right. He hasn't mentioned it openly though. Sergeant O'Shea knows for sure I'd say. He keeps passing sly remarks.'

'Coen still treating you O.K.?'

'Quite well.'

'He's not aggressive towards you?'

'No more than to anyone else. In fact, he hardly ever loses his rag. He's very quiet most times. Why do you keep harping on that? You asked me before, remember?'

'So I did,' replied his father, and was silent.

'Well, what is it? Did he cause 'grievous bodily harm' to a previous assistant, or something. Sergeant O'Shea has been throwing out a few hints as well. But Coen couldn't do anything like that. He wouldn't be kept in the force if he did.'

'What did the Sergeant tell you?'

'Nothing to go on, but I have the feeling he tries to keep all smooth between Coen and myself. I know he likes Coen. Listen, if you know something, tell me what it is. I'm working for the fellow, so I think I'm entitled to know what I'm up against.'

His father thought for a bit. 'It's

nothing against him,' he said at last. 'I found out about it only after you had begun to work for him. A friend of mine mentioned it to me — did I remember the case, etc.? He said the whole thing had gone very deep with Moss, that he had never been able to get over it, and that it might cause trouble later on.'

'Well?'

'I can't tell you any more. If I did, it could alter your whole attitude towards the man, and he'd be bound to notice the change and divine the probable cause.'

'Would that be so bad? I mean, if other people know about it . . .'

'Not so many people know, I should say, although perhaps your Sergeant O'Shea does, from what you tell me.' The Judge smiled. 'We'd better go in; your mother will be coming out to know why we are still here. By the way, I don't know if you mean to tell her what you've just told me, but I should counsel against it.'

'About Geraldine?'

'Yes. When the case is completed and matters have been satisfactorily resolved, then you can bring your Geraldine here and I am sure your mother will be delighted. However, by breaking the news now she will probably suffer needless anxiety, and,' added the elder man with a smile, 'I will be a sufferer also.'

Finny laughed. 'You old humbug,' he said, and put an affectionate arm around his father's shoulders as they walked up the steps together.

Mrs. Raftery, observing from her bedroom window, was much gratified at the sight.

In contrast to Finny's quiet search for information in the well-ordered milieu of the Custom House, Gifford police station, built to accommodate three or possibly four members of the force and in an era when bicycle thieves, school non-attenders and unlicensed dogs figured largely in police prosecutions, Gifford station at this time more closely resembled political party headquarters on polling day.

Large numbers of Gardai came and went. Sheila Curran typed furiously at schedules and reports, and two other typists arrived and were put to work. In the inner sanctum, Moss Coen sifted the data as it came in.

When the day had ended, Moss and the Sergeant went for a walk down to the harbour wall. It was a still June night, hardly dusk even at ten o'clock. Some holiday children still played on the sands, and here and there a sedate couple accompanied sometimes by a dog, measured a steady tread along the water's edge. The sea was as still as the night, hardly sounding at all as it swept in against the shore. The smell of new cut hay hung on the night air and mingled in a not unpleasant manner with the smells of tar and diesel oil and fish and salt water.

Presently, the Sergeant went back to the station, but Moss stayed and sat by the harbour wall, thinking.

Over at the hospital, the night porter admitted a young woman who asked to be allowed to see Mary Purcell. When it was explained to her that the visiting hours had long since ended and that anyway Mary Purcell's condition was such that only very close relatives would be shown to the bedside, she said in that case she would wait, and seated herself in the main hallway, against strong opposition from two members of the nursing staff.

When Garda Noonan arrived there to take up duty for the night, she was still at her post, and having been told by the porter of the reason for her presence, Noonan stopped to have a few words with her.

Thus it was that Moss Coen, brooding as he smoked his pipe and still rooted to the spot where the Sergeant had left him an hour before, was startled to hear the squeal of car tyres and grinding gears coming from the direction of Ship Street.

When he looked around, he beheld the Sergeant running towards him and waving excitedly.

'Come quick, come quick,' O'Shea bellowed, and galvanised into action, Moss got up and sprinted forward.

'What is it?' he shouted.

The Sergeant waited until he was within earshot and then said, moderating his voice, and between gasps: 'Come down to the hospital, sir. Noonan has just phoned. He says he's interviewed a newly arrived visitor for Mary Purcell.'

'Well?' panted Moss.

'He's fairly sure, sir, that the visitor is Lily Sullivan.'

10

When the two men arrived at the hospital, they found Noonan hovering about the lady like a hen with one chick. The girl, a strong-looking, well-made young woman, did not appear in any way upset by their arrival.

Moss said: 'We're police officers, madam. We'd like to ask you a number of questions.'

Lily blinked a little at the 'madam'. 'I'm not leaving here,' she said.

Moss beckoned to the porter. 'We'll need a room to ourselves — can you arrange that?'

The porter nodded and crossed the hall to a narrow door marked 'Office — Private.' He held open the door, and Moss politely asked the lady to accompany them.

She said nothing but put her hand on the back of the chair and made as if to rise. Noonan helped her to her feet.

'I'm stiff from sitting,' she said. She followed him across the hall, Moss and O'Shea coming behind them. Then they all went into the small office and O'Shea closed the door.

The girl sat down rather wearily and turned to face them. Her dark, almost black hair was cut short around her face, which was round and firm; a handsome face without softness or prettiness. To Sergeant O'Shea, who had met her mother, recognition of the daughter had been easy.

'Your name is Lily Sullivan,' began Moss, not wishing to have that denied.

'If you know already, why ask?' Miss Sullivan's voice was sharp and unfriendly.

Moss tried again: 'We want some information about your late fiancé, Simon Connolly.'

Miss Sullivan cut him short. 'Now you listen to me,' she said curtly, but without raising her voice, 'I've travelled a long way to come here and it was for Mary Purcell's sake. She was good to me and I care about her. You get me in to see her, then maybe I'll tell you about Simon. It's

156

stupid for them to say they'll only let in close relatives. She hasn't got any relatives. They won't even tell me how she is, just that she's 'serious'. The newspapers said as much.'

Lily sat back in her chair, her face stony, and Moss, who had had an exhausting day, raised a weary hand to his eyes.

Sergeant O'Shea felt it was time to intervene.

'Miss Sullivan,' he began, 'sure we don't want any unpleasantness, any more than you do. Didn't I myself go down to your family and enquire for you, and wasn't I as discreet about it as anyone could be. And your grandmother will tell you . . . '

'What's my grandmother's name?' she asked suspiciously.

'Why, it's Mrs. Crotty, of course.'

'Are you Sergeant O'Shea?'

'I am indeed.'

'Gran's taken quite a fancy to you.'

With this friendly exchange, the atmosphere became a good deal less intense. The Sergeant looked to his boss for guidance and, finding none, continued on his own.

'All we really want to know is when did you last see this unfortunate young man, and did he seem to be in any kind of trouble or tell you anything which might help us to find out who killed him?'

'And we've a few other questions as well,' Moss growled.

Lily got up and came over to the desk.

'Listen,' she said, 'you can pull a few strings in this hospital, I know, and if you kick up a stink, they'll let me see Mary Purcell. You can come in with me if you like. I only want to see her and to find out whether or not she's going to pull through. Look, I won't say a word unless she speaks to me first.'

'The last we heard is that she is still unconscious,' O'Shea replied in a subdued voice.

'Well, then.'

Moss gave in. 'Do as she says,' he muttered, and as O'Shea framed the word 'how', he turned to Lily.

'If we do this for you, you'll tell us about yourself and Simon; anything which could help us nail his killer?'

'I'll answer every question,' was Miss Sullivan's firm reply.

'Right, then, let's get on with it.'

The hospital authorities, who had decided they did not much care for Detective Inspector Maurice Coen, met his new request with opposition, not to say actual hostility. But Moss, frustrated enough with Lily, was in no mood to tolerate a second defeat, and finding him obdurate, permission was finally granted. Further, he was now told that Mary Purcell was having brief periods of consciousness.

For the second time that day, Moss found himself bundled into a medical gown and mask. In the company of Lily, similarly attired, he once again visited the intensive care unit where Mary Purcell was the only patient. They went in and a nurse came forward and held Lily's arm as they walked across the highly polished floor. Miss Purcell's colour was slightly better and her eyes were open.

Dressed as they were, she could not hope to recognise either of them and

Moss said quietly: 'This is Lily Sullivan, come to visit you.'

The patient turned her head a little and moved her hand. A tube was strapped to her wrist. Lily put out her own hand and clasped the one on the bed.

Mary Purcell said: 'Lily!'

'How are you now — Mary?'

'Glad to see you. Very good to come.'

The effort of speech seemed to exhaust the patient completely and she closed her eyes once more.

The nurse motioned them away from the bed, and they tiptoed out, Moss giving Lily his arm this time. Outside the double doors, another nurse was waiting with the intelligence that 'the doctor' would like a word with Miss Purcell's friend.

Moss hoped his protégée would escape recognition. The nurse stripped off their gowns, and they deposited the disposable masks in a waste container. However, he need not have worried. The man on duty was newly qualified and eager. With an already bulging medical file on the patient, very little of which had been compiled by himself, he was only too pleased to have a listener to whom he could explain the nature of the case in some detail. A chair was brought for Lily and she seated herself with an air of patience, but when he launched into professional jargon, she interrupted and said:

'Look, I just want to know if she's going to live.'

The doctor assumed a superior air. 'It's not that simple, I'm afraid,' he said.

'Well?' she enquired flatly, 'what kind of chance does she have?'

'At this stage it is very hard to tell,' said the medical man, probably quite truthfully.

'Has she a fifty-fifty chance?' persisted Lily.

The doctor hesitated.

'Less than that?' she prompted.

'Yes.'

'A good deal less?'

'As I said, it would be hard to give an estimate. Your friend is a strong woman. Her heart is sound. She was in excellent health when this happened. All that can be taken into account.'

'In other words,' replied Lily, 'she hasn't really got much of a hope, but by some kind of miracle she might just pull through.'

The doctor murmured something about 'not putting it quite like that' but she did not appear to hear him and got up from her chair.

'Thanks for telling me. I only wanted to know the truth. I'll be going now.'

The doctor, who had had time to cast a professional eye upon her figure, shook hands and told her to take care of herself. Moss reflected that of the late Simon Connolly's two women, it was possible that Miss Lovell was the less strong-minded.

The empty corridor sounded hollow under their feet. At the head of the wide staircase, a uniformed policeman stood around. There was no one else about. Moss went over and spoke to him.

'How is our man?' he asked.

'In some pain, I hear. He's O.K. though.'

Moss said to Lily: 'Come with me.'

They went down another corridor at

the end of which a further uniformed man sat outside a door. Seeing Moss, he got up and knocked on the door which was opened from the inside by a second man.

Moss ushered Lily into the room. 'What is this?' she said.

'You told us you'd answer every question.'

'So I will.'

The man in the bed appeared to be asleep. Moss put his finger to his lips and escorted his witness across the room. The light in the room had been dimmed and he said:

'Can you see him clearly?'

He felt rather than saw her little start of surprise.

'I can see him,' she said.

He took her outside again and they heard the door shut and the key turn in the lock. 'You knew him?' he asked quietly, as they walked away.

'I've seen him before, yes.'

'Where? At the post office?'

'No,' she said. 'I never saw him in Gifford.'

'When you met this fellow, were you with Simon Connolly?' As she did not answer, he went on: 'You promised to tell us . . .'

'About Simon,' she countered.

'If it hadn't been for that man and his companion, Mary Purcell wouldn't have been injured.'

She sighed: 'All right, I'll tell you. I hope I'm doing the right thing. His name is Noel Deane.'

'You haven't told us anything we didn't already know. Now be a good girl and give us the information we want. For how long were Simon and Noel acquainted?'

'A few years, I think.'

'On good terms, were they?'

'Oh, very.'

'Come along then, we'll go back to the station.'

'You're not going to question me tonight, are you?'

Moss stopped in his tracks, and turned to face her. 'Even if I had that in mind, I have a feeling Sergeant O'Shea would prevent me.'

She smiled at that. 'It's odd, I don't

remember seeing him at all, when I was working here I mean. And yet I must have seen him around the place.'

'Don't tell him that. He thinks he's a local monument.'

His animosity of an hour ago had completely evaporated. When they came outside, the Sergeant buttonholed him.

'What are we going to do with her? She'll have to find some place to stay.'

'That's so,' agreed Moss.

'I was thinking,' the Sergeant went on, 'Mrs. O'Shea could put her up for the night. That way, few people would know she'd been here.'

'True. Where is your wife going to put her though?'

The Sergeant looked uncomfortable. 'Well, if you wouldn't mind, sir. I mean there's the hotel opposite. They'd give you a room, late as it is.'

Moss laughed: 'I had a feeling you'd make that suggestion. Fair enough. Let her have my room.'

Nevertheless, the Market Cross Hotel did not have his patronage. Instead, the Inspector went for a long walk along the shoreline and then turned away inland. Close to the cemetery, he found a narrow lane, a mud track hardened in this dry weather. On the opposite side of the road to the cemetery, it cut across the fields and bisected the road to Rathnowl.

The Inspector tramped along its flat expanse. Low hedges divided the path from wheat fields on either side. His most constant companions were the young rats scurrying across his path at frequent intervals. He came upon a low building; the roof gone and only broken walls remaining. Known locally as 'the ruin', it was the remains of an ancient stone church. He met no one.

Next morning, saw the Inspector and Sergeant O'Shea seated in the Inspector's office together with the long-awaited Lily. Miss Sullivan looked tired and there were dark shadows under her eyes, but she had lost none of her determination. The proceedings were opened by the Inspector who reminded the witness of her promise.

'Ask away,' she replied in off-hand tones.

'Right, well let's get down to it then. When did you last see Simon Connolly?'

'I saw him on a Saturday; it would have been around the beginning of March.'

'Where was this?'

'At the flat. Simon said he was going home on business and he'd be back within four or five days.'

'What prompted Simon to go away with you?'

'He seemed to have got himself into some kind of a jam. Oh, I know what you're probably thinking,' she went on, 'because I'm pregnant, you think I put the squeeze on Simon to marry me. It wasn't like that.

'I was fond of him,' she added, 'he didn't care about me, though.'

'He did want you to marry him?'

Lily turned to the questioner, Moss, and said: 'We'd been going around together, on and off, for about a year before he took up with Geraldine. He went with lots of other girls too, but when he met her he dropped his own friends. The crowd she went around with wouldn't want to know us, anyway. Then they got engaged, and I didn't see him for a while after that, until one day he came into the shop.

'I said I'd heard he was engaged, and oh, I don't know, he used to get into wild moods sometimes, and he was in one that day. He said he was fed up with working on the farm. When he got engaged, he thought he'd get married straight away, but now he said Geraldine's parents didn't want her to marry so soon, and she'd said she'd wait a while.'

Lily paused, and the two men remained silent. Then she went on: 'He said I'd always understood him, and he cared more for me than for her. I told him if he felt that way, then why didn't he break with her, but he was vague about it, and said it wasn't that easy. Then he went off with himself.

'The following day, he phoned and asked me to go to a dance with him that night. I knew he'd never let go of Geraldine as long as she'd have him. Martin Lovell is a very rich man. I knew that, and yet, well, I was fond of him you see.'

The Inspector made no comment, but waited. However, Miss Sullivan seemed to have ground to a halt.

Sergeant O'Shea coughed, and said hesitantly: 'What about the child?'

Lily turned to him with something like relief. 'That was later; I knew he didn't love me, and it was only because princess Geraldine wouldn't give him what he wanted that he came to me at all.'

'What did he say when you told him about it?'

'Very much what I expected. He worked himself up into a rage, said I'd ruin everything, and he threatened me if I told anyone in Gifford, he'd make me wish I hadn't been born and a lot of other stupid talk.'

'Were you frightened by these threats?' put in the Inspector.

Lily regarded him in some surprise. 'I was not,' she replied firmly.

'You didn't believe he would harm you?'

'No, I didn't.'

'What happened next?'

'It was about a month before I saw him

again. I went home for the Christmas holidays, not saying anything to my people about the way things were. When I came back, I bought myself a wedding ring,' she looked at her hand as she spoke, 'then I went to a doctor in Dublin, and gave a false name. Outside of him, no one knew.'

'When you next saw Simon, what then?'

'It was the end of January. I was beginning to think I might tell Mary Purcell. That was because I'd already got the idea she suspected. But I wasn't sure, and I was just drifting along. I'd say to myself, I'll face it when I have to.'

'What happened at the end of January?'

'Simon phoned me. He sounded very unlike himself. He said he was sorry about . . . you know, the scene we'd had before Christmas. He hadn't been able to think straight, he said. Right there on the phone, he said he wanted us to get married. I told him we'd have to have a talk, and we met that evening. I asked about Geraldine and him, and the answer I got was that he'd finished with her.'

'Did you believe him?'

Miss Sullivan's mouth betrayed a faint glimmer of humour. 'I thought it far more likely she'd put an end to it,' she said in her forthright way.

'You decided to marry Simon?'

'Yes. He was full of plans, so much so I began to believe it was me he'd really wanted right from the start. We were to go to England and get jobs there.'

'Did he give you an engagement ring?'

'No,' she said curtly, 'Geraldine gave him back hers and he sold it so we'd have some money to go away with.'

'Was he short of money?'

'Simon was always short. His mother held the purse strings. Owen used to help him out now and again. I had some money saved, not much, but enough to last a short while. Anyhow, we went over to Holyhead by boat, and then to Manchester. Owen gave us fifty pounds when we were leaving.'

'Fifty pounds!' echoed the Sergeant.

'Gave it to both of you?' Moss pounced on her.

'It was a wedding present to the two of

us, but he gave it to me and said to keep quiet about it until after the wedding.'

'That was very generous of the man,' murmured the Sergeant.

'Since Peter Connolly died, I think Owen feels himself responsible for the family. He's an orphan, a distant cousin, and when his father and mother died, Peter and Maggie Connolly took him in, even though they had small ones of their own.'

'A close-knit family?'

'Oh very. Simon told me that about ten years ago the whole family subscribed to get Owen a place for himself — a small farm. However, after Peter died, he rented it out and came back here to help run the Connolly place until Simon should be old enough to manage for himself.'

'The farm was to be Simon's?'

'I don't really know. Mrs. Connolly has it for her lifetime I think.'

'She is quite a young woman,' Moss said pleasantly.

'She's forty-five,' replied Lily, in the dead-and-buried tones of a girl half that age.

'I was just thinking Simon might have had to wait another thirty years for his inheritance.'

Lily nodded wisely. 'That was partly the trouble. He didn't like work, and he couldn't see himself slaving away at the farm and being his mother's little boy all the time, and the mother is more wrapped up in Brendan anyway; always was, according to Simon.'

'O.K. Fine. Now, you both got jobs?'

'I did. Simon was vague about his though. I don't believe he really had one. At first he seemed very busy, then he went sour and said it was no good and he'd have to go home again.'

'Had you made any arrangements to be married?'

'Yes.'

'And what did you say, when he told you he was going home?'

Lily looked at the two men. 'It's a bit difficult to explain,' she said. 'When he first said we'd go away together, I was delighted. It solved my problems. After the wedding, I could write home and tell the family I was Mrs. Connolly. Then

173

when the baby came, I could hold back that news until a decent interval had passed. However, if Simon wanted to return to Gifford almost immediately, then of course everyone would know about the baby, and on top of that they'd probably say we weren't married at all. So when he began to get restless, I made up my mind the wedding would be where our relatives and friends could see us.' Miss Sullivan's dark eyes flashed.

Moss said: 'After you last saw Simon, did he write to you or phone?'

'No.'

'Were you not anxious at not hearing from him?'

'At first, no. During the second week, I began to get uneasy. But you see, in the meantime something happened. A letter came to me from home, from my mother. I hadn't written in a long time, and I'd had several letters from her, one re-addressed by Mary Purcell. Anyway, in this last one she sounded very upset, and with Simon gone back to Dublin, and no immediate prospect of getting married . . .' Lily trailed away, and then began afresh:

'Well, there it was. Whether or not Mary dropped the hint I don't know, but Ma more or less put it into my mouth to say what the matter was. It all came together, you see. Simon was away, and I was five months gone, and here was my mother writing to say they practically knew and would prefer the truth, no matter what it was.

'I wrote straight away, and three days later my brother, my eldest brother, arrived over. By that time, Simon had been gone nearly a fortnight. I can't explain it, but I had this feeling he was never coming back, and Dan, my brother, when I told him about Simon, he wasn't keen on my marrying him at all. 'You come away home with me,' he said, 'and be thankful if he's left you now. That kind of fellow would leave you even if you married him, and where would you be then with perhaps another child or two as well?' Dan's very outspoken,' she concluded, half smiling.

'You didn't think to write to Simon, enquiring what he was doing or why he

175

hadn't come back?'

'No.'

'You could have phoned him?'

Lily was silent. Then she said: 'I've told you about my brother coming. If it hadn't been for him, I might have done those things. Dan coming, and what he said, put the doubt in my mind.'

'So you went to your own people and they looked after you?'

'Yes.'

'They know you are here now?'

She smiled and flicked the short black hair away from her face. 'Gran knows,' she said. 'Ma and Da will be a bit upset, I dare say. The main thing is that I get home again without being spotted.'

Moss looked at the Sergeant. 'We might be able to help there,' he said.

One way or another, she did not seem too perturbed.

'Would you do something else for us?' Moss asked her.

'If I can,' she folded her hands in her lap. 'What is it?'

'The other man at the post office, the man who was killed; we haven't yet had an identification. His body is at the hospital.'

'You want me to see if I know him?'

'We have a police photograph.' He got up and crossed to the door.

When he handed it to her, she said: 'That's Fonso Quinn; he used to hang round with Noel.'

'Any idea where he came from? Did you know his address?'

'No, I've only seen him a couple of times.'

'And Simon was friendly with these two fellows?'

'Yes.'

Moss said: 'Had you any idea Simon might have been a member of an illegal organisation; the I.R.A. for example?'

Lily seemed surprised. 'I shouldn't have thought so,' she said at once, 'or if he was, I don't suppose he'd tell me about it. And Simon wasn't the type to join anything, and as for handling guns or explosives . . . He'd never want to kill anyone.'

'Yet it turns out that two friends of his had guns and carried out an armed raid.'

She shook her head and said, with an air of finality: 'He wasn't like that.'

Moss got up, felt in his pocket for the pipe, took it out and lit it. He went over to the window and stared out into the sunny street. Two tanned and barefoot children passed by, each clutching a new beach ball. Finally, he turned again to Lily:

'I think that's all now,' he said. 'Our Miss Curran will type up a statement for you to sign, and when you've done that, we'll see about making arrangements to get you home.

'A job for Finnbarr Raftery,' he added, under his breath.

11

The ruin, or to be more precise, Grange Abbey Church, stood atop a small elevation, a slight rise of ground in that flat country, and up this incline Moss and Sergeant O'Shea trudged early next morning. To their right, broad fields of wheat ripened in the June sun, strong and hot even at the beginning of the day.

'Did ye ever see such weather,' remarked the Sergeant, used as he was to the mountainy mists of his native Kerry.

'Sure,' replied Moss, whose bulk made him uncomfortable in the heat.

'I'm glad we got Miss Sullivan away safe,' continued his subordinate. 'Do you know, human nature is a funny thing sometimes.'

'In what way?'

The lines of the Sergeant's face deepened. 'Well now, here's a girl with everything to lose in coming back here, and she makes the journey to see her

179

ex-employer, a woman for whom you'd say she never had a great affection.'

'You think there might be another reason; Deane and Quinn, perhaps?'

'Oh no, the girl seemed very upset about Mary Purcell. She didn't ask to see Noel Deane, now did she?'

'No, it was my idea to have her see him, and she identified him readily enough. You think there's some tie-up between the two things?' Without waiting for a reply, Moss moved across to where a low gateway gave access to one of the fields. He climbed the gate with practised ease and sat astride its top bar. His companion came over to join him, and he watched him lean his weight against a wild blackberry bush.

'Drat the thing,' said the Sergeant, recoiling, as a long shoot adhered itself to his trouser leg. By the time he had disentangled himself, he had forgotten the question, and Moss answered it himself.

'There's a tie-up in one respect certainly. Mary Purcell in her shop and the two Dublin boyos; Simon is the link there. Now that Lily has told us of Simon's friendship with the other two, all we have to do is to try interrogating Noel, and we may clear up thc murder case all in one go.'

'Ye can't do that while he's at the hospital,' objected O'Shea. 'Doctors won't let ye near him except ye talk to him quietly and politely. And what about Fonso Quinn? After all, it was he who actually shot Mary Purcell. Maybe he was responsible for Connolly's death.'

'You could be right,' Moss agreed. 'One thing though, neither Deane nor Quinn appear to have police records, and we still haven't a clue as to why Connolly was killed. However, Mary Purcell has now positively identified Quinn as the fellow who shot her.'

'When was this?'

'Early this morning she recovered full consciousness. Garda on duty was allowed to talk to her for a while and he showed her the photographs of Quinn and got a positive identification, witnessed and all.'

'Will she live, do you think?'

'Well, they seem more hopeful now, although the woman herself asked for her solicitor.'

'What for?'

Moss looked at the Sergeant in some exasperation. 'Why do people usually want a solicitor? To fix up their affairs eh?'

'I was just thinking,' responded the Sergeant, in no way abashed, 'she might be concerned for her own position. She shot a man and killed him, and wounded another. Did she have a licence for the gun, now? No she did not.'

Moss climbed down from the gate. 'Tom,' he said, clapping the other across the back, 'you've a great head on your shoulders.'

The Sergeant looked very pleased.

They walked along in silence for a while, and presently they came to the ruined church, its black stone walls open to the sky. Moss opened the gate and they went inside. Under their feet, the long grass felt soft and spongy.

Of the ruin itself, the roof had long since gone and only three walls still stood, although the remains of the fourth could be seen in the stones scattered here and there. They passed under the romanesque arch of the ancient doorway and found themselves standing on a green mossy carpet. Here the grass was lush and verdant, and was, at that moment, being close cropped by two industrious ewes, who raised doubtful heads to scan the visitors. Having apparently satisfied themselves that the intruders were fairly harmless, they continued mowing operations undisturbed.

The Sergeant removed his hat and scratched his head.

'How did they come in here?'

'Probably from across the road,' replied Moss disinterestedly. 'Let's get to work.'

'Hardly expect to find anything,' remarked the Sergeant gloomily.

'You never know,' replied Moss, 'sometimes a hunch pays off. All along, the main difficulty has been, how did the murderer kill his victim by bashing him over the head with a stone, so that nobody saw or heard, if we presume that no one did? And where did he leave the body while he made the arrangements for burial? Also, if he removed the body to the cemetery unobserved, then he must have had it fairly close by in the first place.

'Last evening, when I was walking I noticed the absence of houses along this track; nothing in fact until you come out on the road to Rathnowl. In this secluded spot, a man could be done away with and no one to know. The body might be left here, and then at a convenient time moved to the cemetery. It's less than a quarter of a mile away. As for the weapon,' Moss paused and waved his hands in the direction of the loose stones, 'plenty of suitable ones around.'

The ensuing hour was spent by the detectives in discomfort and frustration. Together and separately, they climbed amongst the broken walls, examining the ground. It was Sergeant O'Shea who was at length rewarded by the discovery, at the base of the chancel arch, of a broken stone split in two. The Sergeant had noticed this very stone some time earlier, but since then the sun had followed its westward course and now shone in what had previously been a dim corner. The Sergeant knelt upon the grass, and surveyed his find. Gently, very gently, he pulled some grass away from the stone. He called to his companion.

Carefully, the Inspector lowered himself from his perch in the remains of the west wall. The Sergeant proudly pointed to his discovery, and squatted beside it. Moss gazed at the stone, and then joined the Sergeant kneeling on the grass. The two ewes, frightened away by the Sergeant's shouting, returned and resumed their grazing, at the same time closely observing the other quadruped party.

At length, getting up and dusting his knees, Moss said: 'I think you've delivered the goods, Tom. If it's what it looks like, then we've got the weapon, method and all.'

'But no motive.'

'Not yet. Perhaps our friend at the hospital can help us there.'

'Miss Purcell, you mean?'

Moss regarded the Sergeant with good-humoured exasperation. 'Are you kidding me? I mean Noel Deane, of course. Get on down and phone H.Q. now. We'll need all the usual men. I'll hang on here till they come.'

As he waited, he reflected: Simon was chronically short of money. Simon was mixed up with armed raiders. He was subject to wild moods. Was the person who buried him the same person who killed him? Whoever buried him had taken great care of the body. Was he killed for something which he had had in his possession? In that case, who knew of it; Deane and Quinn? If they had killed him, or one of them had, and so come into possession of whatever it was . . . what had brought them again to Gifford, to the post office? Had they taken this object and then failed to dispose of it, as Simon had apparently failed. They had had three months, and here they were still hanging around the very spot.

What had led them to the post office? Lily had told Simon about her work there. Simon told his friends. Perhaps even discussed with them the possible 'pulling' of this job. Was that a motive for the murder? Was he returning to join them in the raid, and had they decided three was one too many. Not much sense in that, but criminals weren't always reasonable or sensible. Just as well, too. Gave a poor hard-working detective a better chance. He'd question Deane, Mary Purcell too. There might be something . . .

Alas for the second part of this intended programme, over at the hospital, death had finally closed Mary Purcell's lips.

When Sergeant O'Shea returned with this bad news, it was to find his superior reclining in the sun, to all appearances asleep, and being closely attended by the two woolly ladies, who were regarding him with what looked like maternal solicitude. The Sergeant coughed and Moss opened his eyes. He smiled good-humouredly.

'I wasn't asleep, if that's what you're thinking.' He got to his feet and stretched himself. O'Shea's expression pulled him up. 'What is it?' he asked.

Tom O'Shea broke the news.

Moss took it well enough. 'That's the luck of the draw,' he said, 'maybe she had nothing to tell us anyway.' He paced up and down. 'The boys will soon be here, I take it?'

'Coming right away.'

'O.K., you stay till they get here. I'm off to the hospital. Deane is going to give me a statement before he has any sudden relapse!'

A little while later, the Inspector was confronting his prisoner. On Deane's normally thin face, new deep lines had appeared. He looked sick enough, and his expression was one of foreboding as he watched Moss seat himself at the bedside, Noonan in attendance.

'Me leg's givin' me hell,' was the patient's opening remark.

'If you will go around shooting up people . . . ' Moss left the sentence unfinished, as Deane sat up in alarm. The movement obviously caused the patient great pain. He clamped his hands to the sides of the bed, and little drops of sweat beaded his forehead.

'I never shot her,' he cried hoarsely.

'Honest, I never touched her. She put the bullet in me.'

'Who shot her; Quinn?'

Deane said nothing but carefully lowered himself into a reclining position.

Moss said briskly: 'Come on, we know it was Fonso Quinn. We've had two witnesses to identify.'

'If you've got witnesses, what d'ya need me for?'

Moss sighed. 'We need a statement full and complete about why you pulled this job, what's behind it, and how you came to plan it in the first place. You could do yourself some good.'

'Oh yeh,' was Deane's rude reply, but he was silent after that, and Moss let him do some thinking. At length the patient said: 'This fellow you say is Fonso Quinn. I want to see him.'

'He's dead.'

'Even if he's dead, he's not buried yet. I want to see him.'

'They've done an autopsy. It won't be too pleasant.'

'Quit making excuses. He's not dead, I know.'

Moss sighed. He had foreseen this difficulty, and had refused to allow the body to be taken to the city morgue. He got up. 'You'll see him,' he said. 'I'll make the arrangements.'

The medical staff were almost equally divided between concern at moving Deane from his room, exposing him to the chill of the mortuary, and distaste at bringing Quinn's dead body to the bedside. Their opinion of Coen, never high, now plummeted to zero. A doctor came in and spoke to Deane.

'The man has been dead for nearly forty-eight hours. Will you not take my word for it?'

'Bring him in,' snarled Deane, in patent disbelief.

The doctor threw up his hands and went out, and soon afterwards an orderly wheeled in the remains of Mr. Quinn. A pad, impregnated with disinfectant, was held over the patient's nose and mouth, and two nurses helped to prop him up so he could see. At a signal from Moss, the orderly took off the covering sheet and, from behind the antiseptic pad, Deane gave a muffled grunt.

Indeed, the staff had been at pains to make the body presentable and the worst of the scars were covered by decent hospital pyjamas. However, the late Fonso's teeth protruded in a way that was undeniably false.

'Do you want to touch the body?' queried Moss of his prisoner. The two nurses looked horrified, but Deane had had enough. He turned away.

'He's dead. I can see that.'

The disinfectant apparently affected his respiratory organs, for he coughed a good deal. When his coughing ceased, he said: 'You got what you wanted. Why don't you get out.'

Moss said: 'You haven't told us anything yet.'

'All right, you wanted me to say that was Fonso Quinn. It's Fonso Quinn.'

'Where did he live?'

Deane said he wasn't saying anything without a solicitor, and Moss said sure, he was entitled. The Inspector went on:

'All we want is the truth. Tell us how you and Fonso came to plan this job and how your other friend came to be involved.'

'What other friend?' Deane asked slowly.

'Simon Connolly, of course.'

The prisoner's face assumed what he no doubt hoped was a blank expression, but the experienced Moss glimpsed the dawn of a new comprehension.

'Don't know any Connolly.'

'And yet, we have a witness says you were very friendly.'

'You and your . . . ' Noonan painstakingly wrote down the stream of profanity.

'Look,' pleaded Moss, 'tell us. You can do yourself some good.'

'Connolly was killed, wasn't he?'

'He was murdered.'

'O.K. So you're looking for the killer still. And along comes nice handy Noel Deane. So you can't find anyone else, and you try to pin it on me.'

'If you're innocent, you've nothing to fear. Already, for instance, we know Connolly went to England to dispose of something, couldn't find a market, apparently got discouraged and returned home. Arrived here on the morning of March 8th. Where were you then, Deane?'

A spasm crossed Mr. Deane's plain features.

12

Meanwhile, out on the road Detective Raftery who had safely and, he hoped, secretly delivered his passenger to her destination, and who was now on the return journey, had been given much food for thought.

The awkwardness of the outward trip had been to some extent got over by Miss Sullivan's matter-of-fact approach and to a large degree by her ignorance of Finny's role in the domestic life of Geraldine Lovell. While not by any means a talkative girl, she had readily replied to what she might have felt to be routine enquiries on the part of an investigating officer, and the picture thus painted of Simon's other fiancée had brought anything but joy to the hearer.

Not having had the benefit of Lily's interview with the Inspector, and of which she was sure he was aware, he heard her speak quite openly about

Geraldine's numerous other 'affairs' as she so unfortunately put it. And one name in particular . . .

However, on the road home, it came to him that he had used his position which was a privileged one, to extract information which he had no intention of putting in his report. If he loved Geraldine as he said he did, then what should it matter to him how many other fellows . . . Unhappily, apparently it did. Cautiously, half-afraid, he probed. Perhaps if he left it alone, it would die a natural . . . No, not that! Think of something else. Mam and Charlie at home. Mam would like Gerry, his father had said so. Like her social position, he meant, that is if she still had one. Surely his mother didn't really . . . What was the matter with him. He and Gerry would live as countless other couples did.

His job called for long hours at a stretch, though. What would she do while he was away? Bored, no doubt. Generally restless, fed-up? He tried to conjure up a picture of Geraldine 'settled' into a domestic routine, and failed. He knew he dared probe no further, but the word loomed even as he shrugged it away; faithful? He lit a cigarette. What did it matter. He was in there now and nothing to do but grab hold and hang on.

Geraldine was still up, when he phoned. He had promised he would. Mrs. Lovell answered the phone.

She said: 'Mr. Raftery? You will let me call you Finny, won't you? Gerry has been biting her fingernails here, waiting for your call. Of course, we are all astounded at the news.'

'What news?'

'Oh, I suppose you are not allowed to talk about it. I'm so sorry. However, I assure you everyone here knows. Mrs. Connolly phoned to tell me. Quite upset and not surprising, poor dear soul, with all she has been through.'

With some difficulty, Finny here interjected the information that he had been away all day, and had only just returned home.

'You haven't heard then?' she said, with a gasp of what could only have been pleasurable surprise. 'Really, I don't know what this place is coming to. Just one shock after another. The latest news is that Rachel Payne has been arrested.'

The silence at the other end pleased Mrs. Lovell quite as much as any loud exclamation.

'Arrested?'

'Well, you know what I mean. 'Helping the police with their enquiries.' Of course she may have been formally charged by now.'

Geraldine, who had arrived at her mother's elbow, took the phone from her. 'Finny, where are you?'

'I'm at home.'

'I've been trying to get you for hours. Have you heard about Rachel Payne?'

'I've heard nothing officially.'

'It's all over the place here that she's been arrested for Simon's murder. Finny, she couldn't have had anything to do with it, believe me.'

The horror of his position kept him dumb. He tried to say something, to steer a middle course, but it was too difficult.

'Finny, are you still there?'

'Yes.'

'Look, I know Rachel; she taught me at school. She's quite incapable of killing anyone.'

In his relief, he broke into hasty speech. He'd ring back later, he said. He had first to make his report, and had just phoned to find out how she was.

Geraldine said quickly: 'I'm fine now.'

'No ill effects?'

'None.'

'I should have enquired of your mother how she is feeling, but she sounds as if she has got over her experience very well.'

'She's quite herself again.'

'Good.'

Impulsively, Geraldine said: 'Oh Finny . . .'

He rang off.

He phoned the Gifford police station to find the Sergeant still on duty.

'Is the Inspector there?'

'He's out, just at present; did ye want him urgently?'

'No. When he comes back, just tell him the trip went off O.K.'

'I'm very glad to hear that.'

'Any news with you?'

'Nothing I'd care to say over the phone.'

'I heard you made an arrest.'

'No.'

'Any prospects?'

'Could be,' replied the Sergeant in his best noncommittal tone.

Earlier, Moss's return to the police station had coincided with the arrival of a special delivery from H.Q. The envelope contained a signed statement, together with an enlarged print of the newspaper photo of Geraldine Lovell and Margaret Connolly, taken on the day of the inquest.

In a vague hope that the purchaser of the blanket might yet turn out to be Miss Lovell, this photograph had been shown to the alert sales assistant, and, incredibly, an identification had been made. Ignoring the two principals, the witness had pointed out a woman shown standing at the back of the group, and Moss Coen, to whom the woman was already known, found himself looking at the neat plain hat and mild plump features of Rachel Payne.

The Sergeant, when shown this piece of evidence, was speechless.

Moss wasted no time. Ten minutes

later, his car drove up at the Payne residence, and shortly afterwards some nameless person witnessed Miss Payne's arrival at the police station accompanied by two detectives. Word spread.

However, when the whole nature of the thing had been explained to the suspect; the blanket found at the grave and the store's identification of her as the purchaser, her reaction was puzzling. She was awkwardly silent.

Moss was trying to make up his mind what line to take, when the Sergeant remarked casually:

'It seems but a short while since ye were at the station last.'

Miss Payne, startled out of her reverie, blushed. 'A most unfortunate affair,' she said, with the return of something like her usual manner. 'I was most embarrassed, and to have to face the Inspector, too.'

'What's this?' cried Moss, astonished.

'Inspector McCracken, sir,' replied the Sergeant, the lady herself being apparently bereft of speech.

'Yes, but what was it about?'

'It was a brooch Miss Payne lost,' the

Sergeant went on, 'only when she couldn't find it, she thought it must have been stolen. Aye,' he continued, 'we went through the usual procedures and with no result, after which Inspector McCracken came on the scene.'

'It was then,' said Miss Payne in a mortified voice, 'that I discovered the brooch where it had been all the time; down in the bottom of my wardrobe; and that is why,' she went on, 'when I missed the blanket, which you quite rightly say I purchased during March, I was reluctant to again expose myself to police . . . well, er, ridicule, I suppose you might say.'

'The blanket disappeared from your house; is that what you would have us believe?' Moss's voice was frankly incredulous.

But in the face of his most persistent questioning, she refused to alter her story. Asked if she had any idea who might have taken it, her answer was, perhaps predictably, no. Two days after its purchase, she had missed it. That was all. She could not recall any visitors to the house. There had been no break-in, nothing had been disturbed. Questioned about the date of purchase, she said it was probably March 12th. It was a Friday, she remembered. And finally, and unbelievably, she offered to produce the store's receipt which she said she had kept.

'I really cannot believe,' she finished up, 'that it is the same blanket found with poor Simon's body. They must have made an error at the shop. One blanket looks much like another.'

Privately, Moss was forced to agree. All the same, rather too much of a coincidence . . . When she had gone, the Sergeant said:

'Ye don't think she did it, then?'

Moss ruffled up his hair. 'Honestly, I can't see that woman murdering anyone. But facts are facts. The blanket is almost certainly hers, and the fellow was buried in her family grave. What we need is motive.'

'She said the blanket may have been stolen.'

'Yes, but look at the problem there. In a place like this, you don't leave a house unseen, not if you've got a large blanket under your arm!'

'Plenty of robberies, even here.'

'Look, if you had a dead body on your hands, would you risk breaking into a house to steal a blanket to wrap it in? Supposing you're caught, and the police begin nosing around and you've still got the body above ground? That won't wash. And the alternative is almost as bad. I mean if the killer knew Rachel Payne; was a friend of hers perhaps.

'Let me put it this way. I come to your house on some pretext or other. I've heard you bought this lovely blanket and I have a dead body on my hands and decide your blanket is just what's needed! Then, with you out of the room . . . '

The Sergeant grinned: 'You ask to use the bathroom.'

'How discreet! O.K. while I'm upstairs, I hunt around, find the blanket, lug it down to the front door, leave it outside somewhere and hope no one notices.'

'It's dark,' put in the Sergeant, 'late at night.'

'Anyhow, you see me to the door. I go out through the gate, and pretend to shut it. You close the front door, and then I creep back, snatch up the bundle, and away.'

'It could be done,' agreed the Sergeant, doubtfully.

'It doesn't make any sense. Tom, do you remember the day of the funeral? We had a discussion that day, and there was something said: to do with McCracken, I think. It crossed my mind when Miss Payne spoke of him.'

The Sergeant looked perplexed, and shook his head.

Moss sighed, and got to his feet. 'Well, no matter. It may come. One thing though — Rachel Payne, we can't let her off the hook.'

'Tonight?'

'Yes, that's rather awkward. I'll ring the Superintendent and see what can be arranged. Anything come out of the watch on Geraldine Lovell?'

'Not a thing. She's not a hundred per cent yet, so I hear.'

'We'll take a chance, then. Leave her alone for a day or two. We can use Raftery there, and transfer the other men.'

Having delivered himself of this ultimatum, the Inspector went out for his late night stroll.

A short time afterwards, Noonan, who had come on duty, interviewed a caller in the outer office. He then put his head round the door and spoke to his superior.

'Sergeant O'Shea; Mr. Connolly wants a quick word with you, please.'

It took the startled Sergeant more than a minute to remember who Mr. Connolly was.

'Owen Connolly?' he enquired.

'Yes, sir, he's come about Miss Payne.'

The Sergeant raised his eyebrows. 'Has he now? Well, send him in and we'll see what he wants.'

The tall, fair-haired Owen entered the room rather hesitantly, and looked around quickly as if expecting to see other occupants.

'What can I do for you?' queried the Sergeant. 'Sit down, won't you?'

Owen said: 'There is a terrible rumour in the town that Rachel Payne has been arrested and charged with murder. Is this true?'

'What!' roared O'Shea, getting out of his chair in a hurry.

His visitor, who looked tired, went on: 'No less than three people have telephoned Mrs. Connolly. At first she did not believe it. She tried to reach Miss Payne on the phone. Finally, I went to the house myself, but there was no answer.'

'This must be stopped,' the Sergeant said heavily.

'There is no truth in it, then?'

'The truth is,' replied O'Shea, marshalling his phrases quickly, 'the truth is that Miss Payne has been kind enough to give us her assistance, and she went home some twenty minutes ago.'

For the first time, Owen smiled. 'I knew there must be some mistake,' he said, with relief. 'Rachel wouldn't hurt a fly.' He gave a laugh. 'I tell you one thing, if you had arrested her, you'd have had my cousin planted on your doorstep by morning.'

'Young Brendan?'

'No, no. Turlough McClintock. He's had a thing about Rachel since they were at college together. He's never got over it.

Still talks about her, although sometimes he doesn't see her for a year or more. Nothing would give him greater pleasure than to figure publicly as her protector.'

O'Shea was thinking how this information would interest the Inspector. He said: 'McClintock's not married?'

'No, he never married.'

Fearing this might prove to be a delicate subject, the Sergeant approached it from another angle. 'Miss Payne is alone now, I believe, except for her sister in New Zealand, so it's a pity they didn't make a match of it.'

'They would have, if it hadn't been for her family. The mother put a stop to it, and nearly wrecked the elder girl's life too. That's how Rachel's sister came to marry this fellow in New Zealand; more than anything, she wanted to get away from her home. There was no opposition to that marriage of course. He had plenty of money, so I heard.'

The bitterness in Owen's voice surprised the Sergeant, who said: 'You knew the family well?'

'No, I heard it from Turlough.' Owen

rose to his feet. 'I must be off,' he said. 'Maggie will be relieved to hear the news. I've left my own place for one night only; going back tomorrow. No sooner had I put a foot inside the door than the whole family pounced on me with this story.'

The Sergeant's agrarian instincts, never far from the surface, were aroused: 'Thought you had your place rented out?' he said.

'The land is rented to a neighbour across the way,' Owen replied, 'part of it anyway. I don't like to rent it all. I'm haymaking at the moment, now that the hay at Moy Farm has been cut.'

'You're a great man for the work,' enthused the Sergeant, and there was a gleam in his eyes which spoke of happy memories of youth. He added, rather wistfully: 'Often wished I had a small farm myself. Telephone Mrs. Connolly from here, if you like,' he went on, 'and while you're on your way home, she can ring her friends and put them right about Miss Payne.'

Owen readily agreed.

13

Moss's evening stroll kept him out later than expected. He covered every inch of Gifford's small streets, made his way out into the country, and delayed his return until about midnight. The night was warm. The air was fresh. At such times, he was content to forget the past.

Not far from the O'Shea home, he paused at the entrance to a Disco. Even at this hour, people were still going in. A few men stood outside, three in a group, none exactly sober, and two others singly, leaning against the wall and smoking. Casually Moss drifted over to the wall, and spoke to one of the men.

''Evening — Reilly isn't it?'

'Yes,' replied the man, and then very quietly added, 'sir.'

'Having a gay time?'

'My party's inside.'

'Shouldn't you join her?'

'If you think that's wise, sir. I felt my

age might make me conspicuous.'

'So it would; you're quite right. For that job, we need sixteen-year-olds.'

The man gave a deferential chuckle at the Inspector's little joke. Moss was about to say he was sure Detective Raftery was with the lady anyway. He wanted to say it, but after a pause he went on: 'Was she accompanied?'

'She came to meet someone. He was waiting for her when she arrived.'

'Do you know him?'

'He wasn't a visitor to the house, at least not while I was on duty.'

'What does he look like?'

'Tall, elegant clothes, smooth patter; you know the type, sir.'

As this description did not seem to fit Finnbarr Raftery, the Inspector received a jolt. 'The lady is supposed to be convalescing,' he said abruptly.

'Just as well it's a warm night, then,' was the cynical reply. 'Get pneumonia in the outfit she's wearing.'

Moss was tired. He'd had a long day and there was a promise of more tedious work on the morrow, but he knew he just had to see Geraldine Lovell's companion.

'I'll move round the corner,' he said. 'Give me the beck when she comes out.'

In the event, this was not for another half-hour. Finally, he saw Reilly throw away the cigarette he'd been smoking. He came up behind him in time to see Miss Lovell step into a sports car. The driver he could not see clearly at first, but then he had a bit of luck. The fellow turned the car, backing onto the pavement as he did so. Whoever he was, Moss was seeing him for the first time. One in the eye for Finny Raftery, anyway, he said to himself.

Just where had he got to in this wretched case anyway? There was no evidence that Simon had belonged to any organisation as a result of which he might have been killed by rivals or 'executed' by his own. Besides, the nature of the killing practically ruled that out.

Fonso Quinn, then. Deane seemed unlikely. And Fonso might have killed him, but who was it had buried him. Not Fonso or his partner, certainly.

That left Rachel Payne, motive unknown, but circumstantially linked with the body.

The grave might have been a random choice, but identification of the blanket had made her a definite suspect.

Next, he had Geraldine Lovell. No tangible evidence here, but motive perhaps yes. Still . . . if Geraldine had been Rachel Payne's age, the woman scorned motive would be more credible. But at eighteen, Geraldine was beautiful, talented and rich! However, not all persons with these assets were self aware, and eighteen was the age of emotional insecurity. Simon jilted her and dashed away to England. Supposing he had written saying he was coming back, intending to take up with her again. Seeing her opportunity for revenge, might she not arrange to meet him up at the ruined church, wait for him in the dark, and then bash him over the head! Melodramatic. And afterwards, remorse, fear too. The body hidden, to be disposed of later (help needed there surely). Rachel's blanket pinched (the mind boggled at that). Still . . . the grave dug, and the body buried with some decency. Yes, with a girl of Miss Lovell's undoubted abilities, just possible.

Next day he was greeted by Miss Curran with a doleful glance and a sheaf of reports.

'What's up, Sheila?'

'I seem to have become a switchboard operator,' she replied with a touch of asperity. 'Noonan has been out twice already, and now there's been a hit and run at Rathnowl.'

'Dead?'

'No. Not that the driver stopped to find out. Someone saw the accident and phoned in. Noonan was off like a hare of course.'

That nebulous unease, of which Coen had spoken to O'Shea, now returned to disquiet him. Something had been done or said that first day . . .

'Sheila,' he said, 'get me Raftery on the phone. He should be at the Lovells.'

Mrs. Lovell, answering the telephone, replied that Mr. Raftery was indeed on the premises, and when told that his superior wished to speak with him, tactfully refrained from mentioning the younger man's presence on the tennis court.

Finny was rather breathless as he spoke into the phone and Moss said (unkindly) that he expected his assistant to keep an eye on Miss Lovell, not to chase after her. The lady was convalescing, he understood?

'She's quite all right now,' Finny said shortly.

'So I understand,' Moss replied, 'and able to be out at all hours of the night, in sports cars too.'

There was a strained silence.

'Recently?' Finny asked at length.

'Last night.' Moss went on: 'That's not why I phoned.' When he had outlined what he wanted, Finny was slow in answering. At length, he said:

'It was something about 'the last time they had an Inspector, he drove them mad with red tape.' At least, I don't think it was the very last time; the time before that, rather. Sorry, I don't really remember exactly.'

Moss scarcely listened. At Finny's first words, the missing piece had clicked into place. No wonder he'd been unhappy. He should have spotted it earlier. A pity

O'Shea was away. However, he'd get it all on the files.

'O.K., Finny. That's all, I think. I've got it now.'

Left metaphorically in the dark, Finnbarr Raftery's mental processes soon fastened on the earlier part of this conversation and he returned to the tennis court in no very sweet mood. Some minutes later, attracted by the sounds of angry voices, Mrs. Lovell hurried to one of the upstairs windows overlooking the garden. Her daughter and her detective friend were standing one on each side of the net, arguing so heatedly that neither could be understood.

A lovers' quarrel! Mrs. Lovell smiled fondly. Presently, the voices came nearer the house, there were sounds of running footsteps on the stairs, and a bedroom door slammed. When Grace Lovell again looked out of the window, it was to see Mr. Raftery sitting alone on the grass and looking rather disconsolate.

She went downstairs. At the sound of her approach, he turned round and got to his feet.

'I'm sorry,' he said. 'I've upset Geraldine.'
He shrugged his shoulders.

'She's told me you want to marry her,'
Mrs. Lovell said.

Finny looked away. 'Yes,' he said, 'I do.'
He sighed, and scuffed a large shoe along
the grass. 'I can't make her love me, if
she doesn't already,' he added miserably.
'I thought . . . well, it doesn't matter what
I thought. Let my imagination run away
with me, I suppose.'

'What is it? What has happened?'

'It doesn't matter,' Finny said.

'It sounds to me,' said the lady, 'as
though it matters a great deal.'

Goaded, Finny said: 'You know she
went out with this other fellow last night.
And in his sports car.' Somehow, the
sports car loomed large in the affair.

'I know nothing about it,' Grace Lovell
said. 'Martin and I were out last night,
and Geraldine had gone to bed before
we left.'

Awkwardly, Finny contemplated his
feet.

'We'll soon settle this,' Mrs. Lovell
walked briskly towards the house, and

216

mounted the patio steps. Finny was reminded of whose daughter she was. They went into the house and he let her go up the stairs alone. He heard her knock on Geraldine's door and there were some muffled noises from within.

'Geraldine!' said her mother, 'open this door.'

More muffled shouts, the sense of which Finny could guess at. In spite of himself, he grinned. His long legs sprinted up the stairs.

'Gerry,' he said, 'don't be an idiot.'

They heard the key turn in the lock, and the door opened a fraction. 'What do you want?' a gruff voice said.

What came over him at that moment, Finny never afterwards knew. He took two strides forward, pushed open the door, and pulled Miss Lovell out onto the landing.

'Listen to me,' he said, 'we've troubles enough without the complication of Kevin Flynn and his wretched car! Don't be such a little fool.'

She struggled to be free of him, and he let her go and turned away, leaving the two ladies silent behind him, the younger one quite open-mouthed with astonishment.

When the Sergeant arrived back at the station, he saw the look in Moss's face.

'You've found something!'

Moss nodded.

'Tell me,' O'Shea demanded, pulling over a chair and sitting in front of the desk, piled high with files and papers. Moss, who had been puffing at his pipe, took it out of his mouth and held it away from him.

'Tom,' he said, 'when we began work, you told me of the last important case you worked on with an Inspector. I asked you if it was murder, and you said murder was suspected. And you said something else: you said, 'the last big affair, not counting Miss Payne's brooch being lost and that was recovered'.'

O'Shea was rather disappointed. 'Well, we know about that,' he said reasonably, 'and you heard all about it from the lady herself. It was never stolen. She just mislaid it.'

'Nevertheless,' Moss went on, 'you

knew something about it which I didn't know, and never thought to ask. I should have spotted it before, and indeed I had a feeling there was something only I couldn't quite figure it out. Noonan put me onto it today, when I heard he'd gone to the scene of a hit and run.

'When I came down here, I took it for granted this was rather a backwater. Typical fishing village, with a few hotels. The kind of place where people never lock their doors. Instead of which, breaking and entering is common, stolen cars, all the usual crime, and now we have a hit and run, not to mention the post office raid. So I asked myself, what was so special about Rachel's brooch? And in the files here, I found the answer; it was valued at five thousand pounds.'

The Sergeant nodded wisely. 'But,' he objected, 'it was never stolen.'

'She said it was never stolen. That's not quite the same thing.'

The Sergeant looked bewildered. 'I agree, we've only her word. But what would be the point . . . '

'I've been looking at the dates,' Moss

answered immediately, 'and they are suggestive. Look here,' he pushed the file towards the Sergeant indicating the spot with his finger. 'Simon Connolly left this town on the 10th February; on the 20th, Miss Payne reported her brooch stolen.'

'Well then . . . '

'She may not have missed it at once. Simon returned to Dublin on the 8th March, with something in his possession which made him shy of prying strangers. The only evidence we have suggests he died on March 11th. And what was the date of Miss Payne's embarrassed visit to the police station to explain about the brooch being found in the bottom of her wardrobe?'

'March 18th,' replied the Sergeant glumly.

'So she finds out who it is has stolen her family heirloom. Lures him away somewhere. Dots him over the head. Recovers her jewellery, and buries the body neatly in the family grave, sewn up in a blanket bought for the purpose.'

'Surely,' objected the Sergeant, 'she'd hardly bury him in the Payne grave. It connects her with the killing straight away.'

'She wasn't to know Jack Finnegan's sharp eyes would spot the disturbance at the grave. Look at it this way,' continued Moss, 'that grave only holds three people, and her parents are buried there already. Her sister is married and in New Zealand. The occupant of the third place could only be Rachel herself. Of course, she'd never think of shrewd Mr. Finnegan or Kevin Bates. She'd figure once Connolly was under the sod, then she'd be safe.'

The Sergeant looked slightly dazed. 'It may hang together, sir, but we can't prove any of it, can we?'

'Not yet,' replied Moss cheerfully. 'Tomorrow I shall pay a visit to a gentleman who invited me to do so 'any time I was passing,' namely Turlough McClintock. And,' he went on, shuffling through his papers and bringing out one for the Sergeant's inspection, 'take a look at this report carefully prepared by our Mr. Raftery.' He popped it into O'Shea's hands and indicated some lines at the bottom of a page:

'Owen Connolly's presence in this country is apparently undocumented; Finny has been unable to locate any registry of birth.'

That night, poor Mrs. O'Shea got little sleep, as her spouse tossed and turned, trying to figure it all out.

14

When next Moss visited Noel Deane, the latter's condition was, according to the hospital staff, 'quite satisfactory.' And his lowered pulse rate was reflected also in an apparent willingness to face the realities.

'What'll happen to me?' he asked the Inspector. 'Tell me — honest?'

'I told you before, you could do yourself some good.'

'Yeh, well . . . sometimes a fella don't know which way to turn. Since then, I heard you were . . . you know, O.K. like.'

Moss wondered who had supplied this information. 'Are you going to tell me or not?' he asked.

Noel heaved a sigh and said, with a show of reluctance: 'What d'ya want to know?'

'About the brooch stolen here in Gifford, earlier in the year.'

Moss expected preliminary denials, but the patient merely looked at him with an expression of foreboding.

'Listen, cop,' he said, 'now you just listen. I never killed Simon. No way did I kill him. What's more, I know nothin' about it.'

Sensing rising hysteria, Moss said easily: 'Did I say you killed him? All I did was ask about a brooch.'

'I had nothin' to do with that either,' responded Noel bitterly. 'That was all Mr. Fancy Simon Connolly's idea.'

'What about Fonso?'

'Am I sorry I got mixed up with him! Look at the mess I'm in here; that woman very nearly blew me into the next world.'

'What about your gun?'

'Not loaded, as you well know.'

'Did you know Fonso's was?'

'Naw. Wouldn't 'a' been caught dead with him if I'd known that. He said the guns were for show, nothin' else.' The irony of these remarks seemed to strike Mr. Deane for the first time, for he added savagely: 'Caught dead with him! Nearly put an end to me, all right.'

'The brooch?' persisted Moss.

'Oh that!' Deane seemed relieved.

'Well, Simon thought that one up. Diamonds, he said. All sounded a bit up in the air, but that was Simon all over; not reliable, d'ya know?'

Moss solemnly agreed, and, encouraged, Noel went on: 'He said this woman lived alone; it'd be child's play, only he didn't want to pull the job himself because the old bags knew him. So he wanted me and Fonso.'

'And did you?'

'Not me,' replied Mr. Deane, virtuously. 'In the end Simon said he'd do the job himself, if Fonso would fix it up to get rid of the stuff. Fonso had contacts.'

'Did you actually see the diamonds?'

'Naw.'

'And Fonso was to introduce Simon to 'a friend', where, do you know?'

'Liverpool.'

'Simon was actually to dispose of the goods himself?'

'Sure.'

'How could Fonso trust him? I assume Fonso was to get his cut?'

For the first time, a large grin of delight spread over Mr. Deane's face.

'Too right, he was. He didn't trust Simon no more than I did. So he made him write down how he robbed this old bags and the dates and everything. Then Simon was to get this bit of paper back when he handed over Fonso's share of the money.'

'Smart thinking,' Moss said appreciatively.

'You're right,' the patient agreed.

'And did Simon bring back Fonso's share?'

'Naw,' replied Noel disgustedly, 'the whole thing went wrong, so he said. If you could believe him, that is.'

'And how did Fonso take it?'

'Livid, he was. He was countin' the days till Simon would turn up. Then he got a phone call to meet yer man. Simon told him the deal fell through, and he still had the diamonds.'

'Did he show them to Fonso?'

'Naw, nor would you or I. Swiped 'em, Fonso would have. And he'd make two of Simon, so there'd be no real argument.'

'Did Simon have a gun?'

'You're joking! That mammy's little boy.'

'He didn't have a gun, then?'

'Haven't I just told you, the . . . ' He paused, and then said a bit sheepishly: 'Oh well, he's dead; Fonso too, God help them.'

'What happened to the bit of paper, the one which Simon had to sign?'

'Don't know. Fonso kept it, I suppose.'

'It wasn't on him.'

Noel regarded the detective with scorn. 'Well, it's not a thing you'd carry round with you. Probably had it put away.'

'At his place?'

'Very likely.'

'And where was that?'

Noel sighed: 'I suppose you'll give me no peace till I tell you.'

'Right,' said Moss, writing it down. 'When did you or Fonso last see Simon?'

'Me; before he went to England. Fonso, the same, as far as I know. He had a message to meet Simon, as I said, but Simon never turned up. That's how he thought of this job at the post office; Fonso I mean. He was so mad at not getting the money from Simon, he remembered Simon's bird used to work at the post office and how Simon clued him in on the routine — all the details. Some details!' Mr. Deane finished bitterly, 'he never told Fonso the woman had a gun.'

'Fonso definitely told you he didn't meet Simon?'

'He didn't say that exactly.'

'What did he say?'

'At first he said he was going to use the paper he had; send it to the police. Then, a few days later, when I asked him if he'd done that, he said to shut up about it.'

'You thought he had seen Connolly?'

'Well . . . '

'How soon afterwards did he suggest the post office job?'

'Oh, about a month. He was planning it for a good while; drove down a couple of times to look over the lie of the place. When Simon got dug up, Fonso said the cops 'd be fallin' over themselves at the grave. Easy as fun, the job 'd be.' Mr. Deane regarded his leg morosely.

Feeling he had got more from this interview than he had hoped for, Moss passed on Fonso Quinn's address for further investigation, and took himself off to Turlough McClintock's demesnes.

That man was unreservedly delighted to see him. The small house bore the hallmarks of a bachelor establishment; its fittings were functional and labour-saving. Moss found himself pressed to stay for lunch.

'I cook for myself,' his host informed him. 'Had a housekeeper once. She died. Can't get anyone to suit now; either they won't work at all, or they fuss the life out of you.'

'Ever thought of marrying?' queried Moss, taking advantage of this cue.

'Oh, er well, there was a time perhaps when I did. Years ago, of course.'

'Miss Payne?'

Moss rather expected an outburst at this invasion of privacy, but Turlough merely looked embarrassed.

'It is not idle curiosity,' Moss pressed him earnestly, 'in fact, it was Rachel Payne I came to talk to you about. Have you heard from her recently?'

Turlough passed a hand across his brow. His embarrassment grew. 'Er, eh, we don't, er correspond; I see her very occasionally.'

'Please be frank with me. When did you see her last?'

'Er, the day of the funeral, when you were with me.'

'Have you heard from her since?'

'No. Is she all right? She's not ill? My God,' he exclaimed, 'the post office raid; she's been hurt! Of course I read of it in the papers, but I thought it was a Mrs. Lovell who was caught in the crossfire.'

'No, no,' Moss replied hastily, 'Miss Payne was nowhere near the post office. She is quite well.'

'I am very relieved to hear that,' Turlough said feelingly. He sat down on one of the kitchen chairs, all thought of lunch apparently banished from his mind. Moss sat down as well, and lit his pipe. Between puffs, he said:

'Tell me what you know of a diamond brooch she has; one worth five thousand pounds. Did you know, for example, that it had been stolen?'

Turlough was once more all attention. 'Five thousand!' he exclaimed. 'It's never worth that, surely.'

'A family heirloom, I understood?' probed Moss.

'Oh indeed. Rachel's mother's . . . ' the gentleman here did some mental arithmetic, 'er, yes, her mother's grandfather bought it as a wedding present for his bride. So it is certainly an antique. Early nineteenth century. But Rachel could have told you that herself. No need to come to me.'

'The position is this,' Moss went on quickly, as he felt himself to be on slippery ground, 'in February last, Miss Payne reported to the police that the brooch had been stolen, and we now believe we have the name of the thief — Simon Connolly.'

'Simon!' Mr. McClintock was aghast. 'But how can you know . . . did you find the brooch or what . . . why Simon?'

'To answer part of your question,' Moss said with a smile, 'Miss Payne now has the brooch in her possession.'

'You recovered it for her?'

'She states that she herself found the brooch in the bottom of her wardrobe;

that in fact it was never stolen, only mislaid. And yet, we have good reason to believe Simon Connolly had this brooch on him as recently as March 8th last.'

Turlough looked thoroughly bewildered, and Moss felt his doubts about Mr. McClintock recede. Unless the man was a born actor . . .

'Dear, oh dear,' said his host rather helplessly. 'Perhaps it may have been another brooch altogether; a trinket. It's hard to credit Simon a thief. Does Margaret Connolly know her son is suspected?'

'Not yet. We felt it only right to have absolute proof. And even then, we hope it may not be necessary to distress the boy's mother. He's dead, and Miss Payne has her brooch back. In fact, our sole interest in this piece of jewellery is in the possibility of its providing a motive for the murder. Men have been killed for items of far less value.'

'Oh yes,' Turlough seemed relieved to be able to grasp at something concrete. Not a perceptive man, Moss felt, but one whose mental processes would get to work when he, Moss Coen, had departed.

'What I should really like to know,' Moss went on, 'is the Payne family background. Since Miss Payne is convinced her brooch was never stolen, I cannot press her for too many (to her) irrelevant details.'

'Of course, of course,' Turlough did not seem surprised at this specious bit of reasoning, 'what would you like to know?'

'I understand the father and mother led a quiet existence and frowned on their two girls mixing with the Gifford population generally, and that Rachel's sister, Clara, married partly in order to escape from this atmosphere.'

'Who told you that?'

'The last part of the information came from Mr. Owen Connolly.'

'Owen? I thought he was working on his own farm.'

'He shuttles to and fro, from what I hear.'

'Maggie will certainly need him,' said Turlough, his mind dropping into a well-worn agricultural groove, from which

Moss knew it would be difficult to extricate him.

'Owen worked here as a boy?'

'In my father's time, yes. A great worker, even as a small lad.'

'An orphan, so I was told?'

Mr. McClintock said: 'I fail to see . . . '

'As a matter of fact,' Moss interposed, 'I was an orphan myself.' He gave a wry smile, and Turlough's hostility vanished.

'Were your parents killed?'

'No, they died; my father when I was four, and mother the following year.'

Turlough nodded sympathetically, and Moss added: 'It's a long time ago now, and I scarcely remember either of them.'

'Other relatives looked after you?'

'My grandmother and my mother's sister until I was nine. Then for four years I was in an institution, after which my aunt married, and she and her husband applied to the courts for custody.'

'Well really!' Turlough exclaimed, 'a very similar story to Owen's. Quite a remarkable similarity.'

'His parents died when he was young?'

'Er, yes. He was here for quite a while.

But it wasn't right. We had a housekeeper then, as I said, but she was an elderly woman. We felt he should have . . . well, that was why, when Peter got married, we put it to him would he take the boy, even for short periods. He said it was up to Margaret and she agreed. In the event, he fitted in so well there, he stayed with them practically without a break. We always felt it was a great kindness on Maggie's part. Few young married women would relish the thought. Owen never forgot it to her.'

'So I heard. To get back to the Paynes, though, may I ask you was there hostility to you as a prospective son-in-law?' (Really, thought Moss, he should react strongly to such a question!)

Turlough, however, made no protest. 'They were never openly hostile, no,' he said. 'In fact, by the time I came on the scene, the father was already dead. Mrs. Payne was a woman of great charm; lived in the past of course. That was partly the trouble. She herself came of a very old family, who considered Payne to be a good deal beneath them. She wasn't a harsh or cruel woman. Quite the contrary. And Rachel loved her.'

'What about the other daughter?'

'Hardly knew her at all. She was only twenty when she married.'

'There was no opposition to that?'

'None in the world. You see,' he said, settling himself more comfortably in his chair, 'he had plenty of money, I believe, but it wasn't exactly that either. Although he was born in New Zealand, his parents had emigrated from this country. His father and Mrs. Payne were second or third cousins.'

'So he was one of the family.'

'Exactly. After the war, the father sent him over here on a visit, and of course he looked up all his relations. I believe the father had some notion of him marrying. Anyhow whatever the truth of that, he met Clara, Rachel's sister, and the whole thing was fixed up very quickly. They got married here and she went back to New Zealand with him.'

'And Rachel never married?'

Mr. McClintock coughed, rubbed his hands on his knees, and finally got up and walked around the room. 'It's very difficult to explain,' he said.

Why he should attempt an explanation at all, and to a stranger, Moss found it hard to understand, but Turlough seemed only too glad to have an audience.

'It was at Clara's wedding that I first met Rachel,' he went on. 'We were both seventeen then.'

'Yes?' said Moss.

'She was Clara's bridesmaid of course and it was a dress wedding with all the trimmings. I have a photograph here. Would you like to see it?'

'Please,' Moss replied politely. He had no idea where this was leading.

'Here we are,' said Turlough, who had left the room for a few minutes. In his hands, he held a thick folder covered with greaseproof paper. He removed the paper and opened the folder to display a large wedding group dressed in the fashions of the late nineteen forties.

Weddings were supposed to be happy affairs, Moss mused to himself, while Turlough identified numerous persons, and if happiness were the requisite emotion, then only two people in the group seemed to display it openly, namely, the groom and Miss Rachel Payne, both of whom looked hugely pleased with themselves. The bride, on the other hand, looked merely cool and self-possessed.

'You're not in this photograph yourself?' Moss asked, having studied each face in turn.

'Er, no,' Turlough admitted. 'We weren't actually invited, we just went to see it. Rachel had a blue dress. Even then, I couldn't think why the fellow had wanted Clara, Rachel was so much prettier. She's lovely there, isn't she?'

'Very lovely,' Moss readily agreed. Turlough McClintock might not see why Clara was the married one and Rachel the spinster, but to Maurice Coen the photograph of the elder Miss Payne told its own tale.

Turlough continued: 'She was still at school then; at the local school, where she teaches now. I didn't call to the house, of course, but every time I was in Gifford, I'd go by the school when the classes were ending and sometimes I'd meet her and we'd just say 'hello'. She was very shy, you know.'

'Yes,' said Moss.

'The following year, she left school and I heard she was going to the University. I was doing Agricultural Science myself. We went to dances and the pictures, and we were in a cycling club. I don't know where we found the time for it all, only,' said poor Turlough, sitting down again and looking very earnestly at Moss, 'I know it was the happiest time of my life.'

If I were a woman, thought Moss, I'd probably be in tears. This has the sound of an epic tragedy.

'And then?' he asked encouragingly.

'Rachel went to work for her teaching diploma. She never told her mother about us, but occasionally she'd bring me to the house as a 'fellow student'. Mrs. Payne was always very polite. We agreed we'd wait five years. Time enough for me to get the farm really organised, for the Da was only too glad to leave it all to me.'

Moss smiled to himself, remembering

Owen Connolly's description of Mr. McClintock senior.

Turlough went on: 'Rachel was keen on making a success of her career. She said too that, after we were married, if we ever hit hard times on the farm, then as a teacher she could always take up her job again.'

'Very sensible,' agreed Moss.

Turlough said, with a note of regret in his voice: 'Well it seemed that way at the time. There was, er, well another reason for delaying the wedding.'

'Yes?' prompted Moss.

'I dare say you will find it hard to understand, you, a city fellow.'

'Oh,' said Moss smiling, 'you mean about the money. I'm not as much of a city fellow as all that.'

Turlough looked relieved. 'Didn't want you to think the Da was mercenary. He wasn't. The money to pay for my education came out of the farm, so naturally he'd expect when I married there would be money from my wife, to er, balance the account, so to speak.'

'I understand the system,' Moss said.

'And Rachel had heirlooms but no cash, eh?'

'Not at all,' was Turlough's vigorous reply. 'Her father's estate did not amount to much, but Mrs. Payne had inherited quite a tidy sum from her side of the family. Without being asked for a penny, she gave Clara a substantial dowry. And at that time, she promised the same for Rachel, always provided of course . . . '

' . . . provided she approved the match,' Moss finished the sentence. 'And she didn't approve of Turlough McClintock?'

'No.'

'Any particular reason why not?'

Turlough seemed to hesitate. 'She took a dislike to me from the very first, and could never be got to alter her opinion.'

'So, what happened?'

'I put it to the Da that Rachel might not have money when we married, but she must eventually inherit some part of her mother's assets.'

'He didn't like the sound of that, did he?'

'He didn't mind too much. Saw the sense of it. All the same, he wouldn't settle up about the land. And without a settlement, we should have been just working for him, and he could have chucked us out whenever he felt like it. Not that he would have, ever. The Da wasn't like that. Anyhow Rachel wouldn't agree to her coming here on those terms. She said we should try to save up some money ourselves.'

'That would take some doing.'

'Certainly,' Turlough said warmly. 'Our total gross yearly income was only about two hundred pounds. She earned three pounds a week, and the Da gave me a pound.'

'How did you make out?'

Turlough gave a rather sad smile. 'Our aim was one hundred a year, and in that first year we did actually manage it. Mrs. Payne didn't expect Rachel to contribute towards the housekeeping, and indeed she even paid for some of her clothes. I was on an 'all found' basis, of course. Anyhow, it was a mad idea. The second year, we saved only about sixty pounds. In order to save bus fares, we used to meet only every second week, and during the week when we didn't meet, we wrote to each other.'

'Eventually you both got tired of all this self-denial?'

'In a way,' Turlough admitted.

'What did you do, take up with someone else?'

Amazingly, Turlough did not even take offence at this. He grinned. 'Some fellows would have, I dare say. With me, there was only Rachel. If I couldn't have her, then that was it. In the end, the Da came to understand, and he would have given us the settlement just to see us married, only it was too late then, and anyway Rachel wouldn't have taken it. She wouldn't accept 'charity' she'd say.'

'And Mrs. Payne never relented?'

'Not she. As the years went by, it was less and less in her interest to do so. Her health wasn't good and Rachel took care of her and nursed her. She died about ten years ago.'

'Surely then?' Moss asked (I sound like a busybody of an old woman, he thought to himself).

'Well, I went to the funeral,' Turlough

replied rather slowly, as if unwilling to delve further into a painful matter. A silence fell between the two men.

'You hadn't seen her for some little time?' probed Moss.

'Not for seven or eight years,' was the reply, not too reluctantly given.

'Nursing her mother and all that, she must have changed a bit.'

'You understand very well,' Turlough said slowly, and looking intently at Moss as if in the belief that since Moss's early life had resembled that of Owen Connolly, his romantic affairs might resemble those of Turlough McClintock, which indeed they did not.

Turlough went on: 'I thought Rachel would be very much upset by her mother's death and being left on her own. Neither Clara nor her husband came over for the funeral; the distance was too great, they said. I was thirty-four then, so was Rachel, and we were still young enough to make a go of it. I thought she'd give me the bend, so to speak, that this was what she had in mind. Instead of which, she seemed completely taken up with her teaching. 'You can't think, Terry,' she said to me 'what it will mean to be able to really devote myself to work again. With Mama so ill, I never knew when I might have to take days off. They've been very kind to me at the school and I mean to make it up to them now'.'

Turlough paused, then said: 'Later, she asked for my advice about Clara's share of the estate. Her mother had made a Will leaving it equally divided between the two girls, and Rachel wondered if she should sell the house, or have it valued and offer Clara half its market price. 'I know she'll accept half the value,' she said to me. 'She wouldn't ask me to give up the house if I wanted to keep it. Besides,' she said, 'it will all come to her children anyway, since there's nobody else'.'

Turlough went on: 'She had no intention of marrying then you see. I didn't say anything, of course. Didn't want to upset her. Told her I felt she was quite right to keep the house if she wanted to. After all, it was her home.'

'Oh quite,' Moss said. 'Her sister obviously accepted this plan?'

'I never heard she made any trouble about it.'

'No rift in harmonious relations?'

'Oh nothing like that. The Paynes are a very nice family.'

'So I'd heard,' Moss answered politely.

Turlough suddenly remembered his duties as a host, and seemed genuinely disappointed when Moss felt it necessary to decline the proffered meal on the plea of having already overstayed his allotted time.

Turlough said: 'Hope I've given you some idea of the Payne family. Don't suppose you wanted to hear about my affairs. Trouble is, don't see too many people here. Get a bit carried away, sometimes.'

His visitor grunted something appropriate and shook hands as they parted.

Maurice Coen was not one of those men who 'understand' women. However, on this occasion he congratulated himself that his ignorance of their mental processes was not such as Turlough McClintock's appeared to be.

15

When he got back to Gifford, the Sergeant was waiting for him.

'How did you get on?' Tom asked eagerly.

Moss dropped impedimenta carelessly around the office and went over to his desk. He sat down wearily.

'Tom,' he said, 'what have we got here?'

Assuming this remark to be merely rhetorical, Sergeant O'Shea made no reply.

'Firstly,' continued the Inspector, 'there is Geraldine Lovell.'

'Ye don't still suspect her?'

'I do, Tom. Without the smallest shred of evidence, I do still. But evidence is what we need to bring this case into court, and the blanket, brooch and the Payne family grave, all tangible evidence which may be produced for the jury to see, or sworn to by good reliable witnesses, all that points to one person only — Rachel Payne.'

'Did Mr. McClintock tell ye anything?'

'Two things which are important, I think. One that this brooch was the gift of Rachel's great-grandfather to his bride, which means it must have been in her family for well over a hundred years. But the second piece of information is even more pertinent. Rachel Payne was in love with Turlough McClintock, and for all we know, perhaps she still is. Only lack of money prevented the marriage, and the sale of that brooch would have paid her dowry a couple of times over.'

The Sergeant shifted uneasily in his chair, but Moss went on: 'Here we have a woman of forty-five, her one love affair gone sour. A woman whose family have lived a great deal in the past, hugging cherished possessions. Without any doubt, young Connolly stole that heirloom, and took it to Liverpool, where he attempted to dispose of it. For some reason we don't know of, he failed. He returned to this country and we think he had it with him. Ten days later, Rachel reports to the police that her brooch has been found.

'I tell you,' Moss went on, getting up and pacing across the room. He turned and looked straight at the other man. 'I tell you, Tom,' he said, 'if I can find one person who will swear to that brooch being in Connolly's possession when he landed in Dublin, then Rachel Payne is under arrest.'

'You'd never get a conviction,' said the Sergeant.

'Oh, I know,' Moss agreed gloomily. 'Her counsel has only to put her in the witness box. We saw her at the inquest. Very hard for any jury to believe such a woman capable of murder.'

'I wouldn't believe it myself,' said the Sergeant.

'Well then,' Moss muttered. He put his hand up to his eyes, and went on with a sigh: 'Quite a few things struck me as being peculiar. For instance, Rachel said the brooch was found in the bottom of her wardrobe. That of course may be a lie, but if it is the truth, then she must have thought she left the brooch pinned to a dress or a coat, and it fell out. And she strikes one as such a careful and precise person. It seems odd that she wouldn't take greater care of an article of such value.

'Next, Turlough McClintock said Mrs. Payne took a dislike to him, which she could never afterwards overcome; why? Nothing is known against the McClintocks, and a one hundred acre farm in the midlands, supporting thirty dairy cows, not to mention the sheep and turf; all that would have given Rachel security, one would have thought. And whatever prejudice the old lady had against Turlough, Rachel knew of it even before she brought him to the house. She was careful to introduce him to the mother as a 'fellow student'.'

The Sergeant looked blank, and Moss switched to another line: 'Then we have the problem of the brass plate. Who had it engraved and collected it from Mr. Poddle? He was positive no woman did.'

O'Shea cleared his throat. 'The whole thing about the brass plate is daft,' he said. 'What murderer would bother hanging about the place, fiddling with brass plates. If you murder someone, your whole idea is to prevent any connection between yourself and the deceased.'

'For that matter,' said Moss, 'why dress him up for burial? He was laid out in his best suit and wrapped in a new blanket.'

'So,' finished the Sergeant, 'we come back to your first idea; he was buried by one person, after having been murdered by someone else. Wait a minute,' he went on in a new excitement, 'it makes sense, no it does really,' he protested.

'Take your time,' Moss said, 'I'm all ears.'

The Sergeant went on emphatically: 'Turlough McClintock finds out Rachel has killed young Connolly. She confides in Turlough. Owen Connolly said himself if we arrested Rachel, we'd find Turlough on our doorstep first thing. He also said nothing would give Turlough greater pleasure than to figure as Rachel's protector.'

Moss nodded, a little absently. 'Go on,' he said.

O'Shea's confidence increased. 'Turlough agrees to bury the body secretly. Rachel's parents' grave is chosen as being the safest spot. Rachel goes to town and buys the blanket.'

Here Moss interrupted: 'Why buy a blanket? Why not one already in use, or indeed, why bother with it at all?'

'Simon was Turlough's cousin. He wants to bury the fellow decently.'

'Where did he get the clothes?' asked Moss.

The Sergeant had a brainwave. 'Simon had his suitcase with him, when Rachel Payne met him.'

Moss grinned appreciatively. 'Not impossible,' he admitted. 'I wonder what became of the suitcase, though? Hasn't turned up so far.'

Ignoring these interruptions, O'Shea continued: 'At night, Turlough wraps the body in the blanket . . . '

'Where?'

The Sergeant hesitated. 'In the old church, I suppose.'

Moss laughed, and the Sergeant looked put out. Moss said: 'I'm thinking of Turlough sitting on the grass inside the ruin, and sewing away by moonlight. If he had nerve enough for that, then he's capable of almost anything. I shouldn't have thought he'd have the nerve, though.'

'If Rachel was in danger, who knows what he'd do.'

'Yes,' Moss agreed, 'that's true. Well, we'll get Mr. Poddle to see if he can identify Turlough. I'm sure Poddle will co-operate. And that business of Owen Connolly's birth certificate. We'd better have that checked out. Finny may have made a mistake. How is he making out at the Lovells by the way?'

'So, so,' replied the Sergeant. 'He phoned around one o'clock saying Miss G. had spent the morning in bed and he was browned off hanging around doing nothing. Her mother had asked him to lunch.'

'They seem to like him,' Moss said quite mildly.

'I believe Grace Lovell's father and Judge Raftery were friends once.' The Sergeant's tone was wary.

Moss looked up, seemed about to say something and then apparently changed his mind. When he did speak, it was on another matter. 'Any news from the lab. boys yet?'

'Not yet, sir. They've promised it for five o'clock at the latest. All we've got so far is that the blood traces match Connolly's. Lucky the weather's been fine lately.'

Moss nodded, and looked at his watch. 'Four-thirty now,' he said. Just then, his phone shrilled.

Noonan, in the outer office, put the call through. 'Detective Raftery, sir,' he said. There was a click.

'Moss here,' said the Inspector. 'Yes, Finny, go ahead, what is it?' Tom O'Shea could not hear what was being said, only the sound of speech on the line. The Inspector's face changed and he got to his feet. He let the speaker continue uninterrupted, but watching him closely, the Sergeant felt he had seldom seen a more ominous expression.

At length Moss said curtly: 'Stay where you are; I'm coming over.' He put the phone down, cutting off the reply. As he made for the outer office, the cold blue eyes never looked more dangerous.

'What is it?' asked O'Shea, following him.

Moss did not answer, but opened the door. 'Sheila,' he said, 'get on to Headquarters. Have them put out an alert. I want every man they can spare. Miss Geraldine Lovell has made a run for it.'

The Sergeant exclaimed, and even quiet Noonan jumped up from his chair. Miss Curran was already briskly dialling. 'Description?' she asked.

'Last seen in her pyjamas,' Moss replied savagely. 'Possibly now wearing pale blue jacket and navy slacks. Height; five feet seven inches. Red hair, blue eyes, slim build. She's had anything from ten to fifteen hours start,' he added, 'and she's taken her father's yacht — the *Emer*. Or, at least we must presume she has. It's missing.'

He turned to the Sergeant. 'Tom,' he said, 'I'll leave you to co-ordinate things here. If there's any news, contact me at Lovell's. I should be back in thirty minutes or so, when I've seen the situation there for myself. If Martin

Lovell arranged this escape, then we're in for a long hunt. However, for what it's worth, that idiot Finny seems to think he knew nothing about it.'

The Sergeant, who was already busily phoning, motioned Noonan to accompany the Inspector.

'Take Noonan, sir,' he said.

'Right,' said Moss, 'come on.'

He and Noonan ran out to the car, and about five minutes later they drew up at Furry Park House.

Finny was waiting for them at the front door. As the car stopped, he came out to meet them. Though almost blind with anger, even Moss could see disaster in every line of Finny's lanky body. For some reason, he was unable to look at the face, and that fact hurried him into recrimination, unpardonable in front of Noonan. He opened the door and got out.

'Well,' he said, 'you've let her slip. While Sergeant O'Shea took on more than his fair share of the work, you were lazing around here; the only job we could give you, and even that you've bungled!'

Still in the car, Noonan looked very uncomfortable. Finny said briefly: 'Martin Lovell would like to see you at once. He's afraid something may have happened to his daughter.'

An explosive sound came from Moss. 'Afraid something may have happened to her? Is he indeed! Just wait till I have a few words with Mr. Lovell!'

The two men met in the hallway, Martin having heard sounds of the Inspector's arrival. Geraldine's father was the first to speak.

'I'm glad to see you, Inspector,' he said. 'Won't you come inside, please. There's a lot to be done and we've very little time.'

Moss held up his hand. He was making a tremendous effort. Any moment now, he thought, and I'll be foaming at the mouth. An ally appeared in the shape of Mrs. Lovell, always a pourer of oil on troubled waters. Her distress was tangible, almost an all-pervading horror. She knows what this means, thought Moss, and the awareness sobered him. Either Martin Lovell didn't know, or he was acting a part with complete conviction.

Moss said: 'Better get the facts straight. Who was the last person to see your daughter?'

They remained standing in the hall, and Mrs. Lovell said: 'I imagine I must have been the last to see her.'

'When was this?'

'About one o'clock this morning. Martin and I had just come in. Martin went straight up to bed, but I went into the kitchen to heat some milk. Geraldine, who had gone to bed much earlier, must have woken up at our arrival, and she came downstairs in her pyjamas and got herself something to eat, while I was having my milk.'

'Did she say anything?'

'Not very much; just trivial conversation.'

'For example, she didn't say she was leaving home and wouldn't be back!'

Mrs. Lovell's hands fluttered in an agonised movement and Martin pounced on the Inspector. 'No need to upset my wife with that kind of remark,' he said sharply.

'I'll re-phrase the question,' Moss

continued grimly. 'Mrs. Lovell, did your daughter's speech or actions in any way suggest to you that she might be going away?'

Grace Lovell hesitated: 'She was rather subdued. However, at that hour of the morning, I was quite sleepy myself.'

'Was there anything unusual in her manner towards you?'

'She was a little more conciliatory, perhaps. We had had a row the day before and were being extra nice to one another as a result.'

'What did she have to eat, did you notice?'

Mrs. Lovell again hesitated, and Finny said in a rather strangled voice that he understood Miss Lovell had consumed sandwiches and some left-over apple tart.

Moss turned a baleful eye in his direction. 'Thank you, Detective Raftery,' he said. 'In other words, a substantial meal. Did she take any food to bed with her?'

'I don't know,' Mrs. Lovell replied quickly. 'I went up first, you see.'

'She said good-night to you?'

'Yes,' Grace Lovell swallowed, then went on: 'She said she was very tired and would sleep late in the morning. She asked me to tell Bridget not to call her or bring her any breakfast.'

'What happened this morning?'

Here Martin intervened. 'We've been all through this, Inspector. The thing is to find Geraldine as quickly as possible. You don't understand . . . '

Moss was in control of himself now. 'Just a moment if you please,' he said. 'A full scale alert is already under way. The answers to these questions may provide us with the clues we need. What happened this morning?'

'Nothing happened this morning,' Mrs. Lovell replied with some asperity.

'Nothing?'

'Mr. Raftery came of course,' she said, with a glance of approval at poor Finny.

'What time was this?'

'About eight o'clock,' Finny said.

'Hardly the time for a social call,' Martin Lovell growled.

'Please dear,' Mrs. Lovell sounded gentle but firm.

Moss transferred his attention to his subordinate. 'Did you enquire for Miss Lovell?'

'Yes. I came round to the back door. Didn't want to wake the whole house. Bridget was in the kitchen, and then Mrs. Lovell came in. She offered me some breakfast, but I said I'd already had some. She told me Geraldine had said she would be sleeping late, so I said I'd come back around eleven.'

In the presence of the Lovells, Moss could hardly ask if Finny had had the house under observation during that time, so he assumed the answer to that one and enquired what had occurred at eleven.

'When I returned,' Finny said, and his dejection showed in his tired voice, 'Bridget answered the door. She said Mrs. Lovell had gone out, but had particularly asked that I should make myself at home. Bridget put me in the sitting-room and brought me a cup of coffee.'

Grace Lovell gave a deprecatory cough. 'At twelve o'clock,' she said, 'I found Mr. Raftery still here and no sign of

261

Geraldine. And I said to him I'd give Miss Lazybones a call.'

'And did you?'

'Certainly. I knocked on the door. There was no answer. Then I tried the handle. The door was locked.'

At this, Martin Lovell and Finnbarr Raftery broke into confused speech. Neither could be heard and Mrs. Lovell's sedate tones continued:

'My daughter and I had had a row on this very subject the day before. I had made it clear to her then that I did not wish her to lock herself away for hours at a time. However,' Grace waved an airy hand, 'so much was said on that occasion, I really didn't wish to provoke another storm. I came downstairs and told Finny she would be up quite soon, and he had better stay to lunch.'

'When one o'clock came and there was still no sound from her room, we became anxious. I tried the door again and we went outside and looked up at her window. It was open. Her father came in just then, and Mr. Raftery fetched a ladder and climbed into the room.'

'It was empty,' Finny said, 'and there was no sign of any hurried departure. The bed had been slept in.'

'Was the key in the lock?'

'No. I couldn't open the door. So I came back down the ladder again.'

'Mrs. Lovell,' Moss said, 'may I see the room please?'

'There isn't time for that,' Martin broke in impatiently. 'She's taken the *Emer*. Don't you understand?'

'She handles it well,' Moss replied coldly.

'Inshore, yes.'

'You think she may have taken it out to sea?'

'Martin eyed him with revulsion. 'I don't know where she may have taken it. There's a sea mist forecast for tonight, and it's now nearly five o'clock. Don't stand there talking about it. Do something.'

If Martin Lovell was acting a part, then he was doing it superbly. Mrs. Lovell, Moss noticed, seemed less anxious about her daughter's chances on the open sea.

Moss said grimly: 'Believe me, sir, we'll

have a helicopter on the job if it's necessary. If we had received notification of her absence three hours ago, then your daughter might have been found by now.' He looked at Finny as he spoke, but Martin took the remark personally.

'It took a while before we discovered the *Emer* was gone,' he said. He didn't seem to find this police concern out of place.

Mrs. Lovell said quietly: 'I'll show you the room, Inspector. We found a duplicate key.'

Moss walked to the foot of the stairs, and Finny made as if to accompany him. Moss noticed the move and turned to him. 'I shan't need you here,' he said shortly. 'Get back to the station, and don't get in the way of the Sergeant. He has enough on his hands.'

Mrs. Lovell was already on the landing above, and without waiting for an answer Moss hurried after her.

Martin Lovell regarded Finny in a more friendly light. 'Your boss seems a bit upset,' he said.

'I know,' Finny said miserably, 'he's

blaming me because I didn't notify the station earlier. I blame myself too. Only at first I was sure we'd find her. Never thought it could be serious.'

'Neither did I,' Martin agreed. 'She's full of spirit, that girl. Always up to something. More like a boy than a girl, really.'

Finny could hardly agree with this last sentiment, but he finally said it was true he hadn't known many girls like her.

'Even now,' said Martin, 'she'll probably be all right. Plenty of common sense. Not like her to take off out to sea. The *Emer* isn't built for that and Geraldine knows it. Tell you what,' he added confidentially, 'if the Inspector doesn't need you, why not come with me. Some of the fellows in the yacht club are going out to search for her. A friend of mine said he'd wait for me till the police were finished here. What is the fellow doing up there?'

Like a caged tiger, Martin paced across to the foot of the stairs.

'Grace!' he called. A few seconds passed and Mrs. Lovell's head appeared over the banisters. 'Grace,' he said, 'I'm off. If the Inspector should want me, tell him to contact the yacht club. They'll know where I am.'

'Be careful, Martin,' she said, a little tremulously.

'Sure thing,' he replied. 'Don't worry, we'll get her.'

Mrs. Lovell returned to the bedroom, where the Inspector was making a thorough search, not that he hoped to find anything. His opinion of Miss Geraldine Lovell differed but little from that held by her father.

Mrs. Lovell said: 'My husband has gone down to the harbour.'

The Inspector, now deep in the recesses of the wardrobe, gave a grunt. He scarcely heard the soft purr of Martin Lovell's big car as it pulled away from the house.

'Did you find anything?' Mrs. Lovell's anxious voice reached him.

'No, not a thing,' he said, re-emerging to confront her. 'Not that I expected to,' he added with a sour face, 'but we have to do these things in a routine fashion.'

'Oh, I understand you want to do everything to find her,' Mrs. Lovell's hands fluttered again. 'I'm afraid my daughter is causing a good deal of trouble.'

Moss sighed wearily. 'She is indeed,' he said.

'I'm afraid, Inspector, she has always been, well, rather difficult.'

'H'm,' he said grimly, 'if she had had the benefit of my education, a lot of that would have been knocked out of her.'

Mrs. Lovell's eyes read his, shrewdly he thought. But she took his remark at its face value. 'At one time we did try a boarding school,' she said, with a half smile. 'I believe the nuns were quite strict. However, after only two terms, the Reverend Mother wrote and said perhaps it would be better if we did not send her back there. Geraldine, she said, did not quite 'fit in'.'

'I can imagine,' was Moss's only reply.

Back at the police station, for the second time in a week, pandemonium had again broken loose. Finnbarr Raftery now sailing out of Gifford harbour, need not have worried that his absence would be remarked upon. Four or five other members of the force could easily have been overlooked in the crush. Numerous reports reached Gifford of unidentified yachts and dinghys but, as the evening wore on and the all-pervading mist closed in, one by one these mystery mariners returned to port and were accounted for, until, by about nine o'clock, only six remained outstanding. One of these was thought to have been a duplicated report, which could not now be checked, and another appeared to be unaware of the danger until about two hours later when she began sending up distress flares and the local lifeboat went to her assistance.

But before any of that happened, Moss and Tom, closeted in the inner office of Gifford police station, were endeavouring to keep pace with a flood of reports.

'Everything comes together,' grumbled Moss, fingering with distaste a many times folded and well-worn piece of paper. Pursuant to Garda enquiries, it had been found in a seedy bed-sitting-room, the erstwhile domicile of the late

Fonso Quinn. Sparsely worded, it confessed to the taking of Rachel Payne's brooch from her house on January 28th. The signature was that of Simon Connolly.

'This provides motive, if you like,' the Sergeant said. 'Supposing Fonso Quinn was blackmailing Simon, threatening to use this against him. They meet up at the ruin, and Simon tries to get rid of Fonso, but Fonso is bigger and tougher and kills Simon instead. How's that?'

'I'd buy it with pleasure, if it were not for the burial. Tell me Fonso Quinn bashed Simon over the head with a rock, and I'll believe you. Tell me he took him away and buried him in Rachel Payne's blanket . . . There's intimate knowledge there, Tom. Whoever buried Connolly is a thousand light years away from the mentality of Fonso Quinn.'

Noonan put his head round the door. 'A messenger here, sir, with a lab. report.'

'Now they send it,' groaned Moss. 'Right, Noonan, let's have it here.' He perused it slowly, and then, without a word, passed it to the Sergeant, who finally exclaimed:

'I don't believe it!'

Moss said: 'Have we still got a case, Tom?'

For once, the Sergeant was at a loss. He said, hesitating: 'D'ye think this rules out Rachel Payne altogether?'

A weary Moss said: 'Go away, Tom. Let me think.'

As the door closed behind the obedient Sergeant, Moss pulled a sheet of paper towards him.

He wrote rapidly, filling the whole sheet. At the head of the paper, he put down 'Five thousand pounds' and circled it. Diamonds were forever, weren't they? And five thousand pounds worth of heirloom, that was the big factor. Then there were others. Lily's baby, and Clara Payne's wedding photograph. He could cable New Zealand, if he had to. Still, proof could be got nearer home . . . a chance remark of the Sergeant's came back to him . . . Social Welfare? He dismissed that . . . no, wait a bit, it was something Lily had said; 'about ten years ago.' Registry of Deeds, that was where to look. Oh yes, and it fitted in so well with Clara and Rachel agreeing to split the value of the house. No doubt a few pounds had been squeezed out of that transaction to benefit the third party, and Clara Payne's husband none the wiser.

He lifted the phone. Proof he could get later. He had to act now. He might still be in time. Although he rather doubted it. Miss Lovell had been too clever for that, he felt.

16

Martin Lovell said: 'Can't see a thing in this mist!'

Away to his left a voice said: 'We're on course.'

Finny, in borrowed oilskins, peered out into the gloom. It was not yet dark, but visibility was down to five yards. His nose was clogged and his fair hair, curled up with the damp, hung with beads of moisture, which now and again dropped rivulets down his face. In his hand, he held a loud-hailer into which he bellowed every so often. He had been doing that since the mist descended about an hour before.

When first they had left Gifford, they had sailed straight out to sea to catch up with the other two boats. All three had then followed a course parallel with the shore. Nothing had come of that, and after an hour or so, they had put about, sailing back until they again met Gifford's beaches.

This had led to their meeting with the *Dun Mhuire* trawler, just out of Gifford harbour and headed for the open sea. Her master said he had come to join in the search. He gave them his proposed course which he said he would continue to patrol, and when he heard Martin Lovell was present, he offered to take him on board. In the end, Martin declined the offer. They were beginning to get very anxious indeed; even Martin who had been fairly optimistic at the start.

Finny said: 'You'd think the lifeboat would be out.'

'She is already,' said one of the men.

It seemed to Finny he had shouted himself hoarse when the sound of a foghorn and an engine close by, heralded the return of the trawler. He hailed the ship, which showed full lights. Even at a few yards' distance, she merely gave off a dull yellow glow.

The master seemed relieved to see them. 'Afraid we'd run you too close,' he said. 'We're packing it in. Weather's too bad. Can't see anything till you can almost feel it. Might do the girl an injury.

If she's hove-to and keeps her head, she'll be all right. No wind to speak of.'

The trawler chugged away, and they were left alone again. Presently, they heard the distress rockets fired, not too distant, they judged, although they could not see. Making some hasty calculations, they altered course. Then they could hear shouts, carrying on the still night air, but distorted by the mist.

'It's the lifeboat,' Martin said jubilantly. 'They've got her!'

But of course it was not his daughter: merely two foolhardy yachtsmen who had hung around believing the mist would clear, and had then lost their bearings. By this time, the owner of the boat was becoming restless.

'We're doing no good this way,' he said. 'The girl may have been found by now. We should go back. If she has not been seen, then we will go out again in the morning.'

Martin looked dejected, and Finny tried to cheer him, although the younger man was himself in the grip of a depression.

'She'll be all right, sir,' he told her father. 'Like the trawler skipper said, there's no wind forecast.'

'If she's all right, then where is she?' Martin asked. 'She must have seen the mist descending. Why didn't she make for home before it grew dark?'

It was then that the first mention was made of Blue Island. The owner of the boat suggested it, but Martin rejected the idea. 'It's thirty-five miles away,' he said, 'and ten miles off the coast.'

'Well, she's been gone so long,' the other said, 'it's quite possible.'

'Oh, possible, yes, but what on earth would bring her there?'

'It's a place anyone might go to. She may not have been able to get back.'

'If so, at least she'd be safe,' said Martin, and there was a note of relief in his voice.

'Let's go back to Gifford,' the boat owner said. 'If she hasn't turned up yet, we'll drive down the coast and put out from Windy Harbour. We can hire a boat there.'

This action was decided upon without

any reference to Finny, who indeed felt so numb from the damp and his fears that he was glad to be left out of their counsels. The skippers of the two boats in their wake were duly advised of this change of plan, and without demur they all made for home. Nearer the shore, the mist was not so dense, and they reached harbour safely.

It was about this time that Maurice Coen recalled the existence of Detective Finnbarr Raftery. The Inspector and Sergeant O'Shea were back in the inner office together. Another alert had gone out, this time to check on passengers leaving by sea or air. The last passenger sailing went at 10.15 p.m., air travellers were already subjected to some scrutiny, and few trains ran after 11 p.m., none of them leaving the capital. In short, thought Moss, we've plugged the holes now, but it's far too late surely. Twenty-four hours too late.

He cursed himself for having been a fool. He should have seen the whole thing long ago. The motive he could only guess at. Five thousand was enough of a motive in anyone's money, but he had a feeling it went much deeper. Not that they'd prove murder now. Very likely, thought Moss, it wasn't murder. Manslaughter then.

To have been so close, and then to have it slip through his fingers. In a natural progression of thought, much of the resentment thus engendered smouldered and finally settled on the shoulders of the hapless Finny. If Raftery had done his job, then they should have had six, possibly nine hours extra, and events might have taken a very different turn.

'What did you do with Raftery, Tom?' he said to the Sergeant. 'I sent him back to the station at five o'clock. Did you pack him off home?'

The Sergeant was quite scandalised. 'I didn't do anything with him, sir. He's not responsible to me, as you well know.'

'Well, when he turned up here, did he go off duty, or what?'

'I've really no idea,' said the kind-hearted Sergeant, pretending to be huffed. 'I'd quite enough on my plate at the time.'

Unfortunately, this remark awoke a

fresh sense of grievance. 'I know, Tom,' growled Moss, 'you've had more than your fair share to do, and all because of that loafer. Well, one thing is certain. This case may have gone against me. At the beginning, I admit I had no great hopes of it. But I'm going to settle Mr. Finnbarr Raftery's hash for him. He'll be lucky to escape the charge of collusion.'

The vivid blue eyes had reduced themselves to slits, and the nostrils were stuck together. Looking at the strong broad fists now thumping themselves one into the other, Tom O'Shea was glad of Finny's absence.

He hesitated. He would have liked to withdraw quietly from the situation and hope it would resolve itself. Moss was not a cruel man, and no doubt Finny had asked for it. All the same, the Sergeant had the feeling he was being called upon to mediate, and he was not a man to turn his back on human distress.

Moss, who had got up from his desk, was looking out of the window. The Sergeant remained seated, crossed his legs, and said conversationally:

'You've had it in for him, right from the start, haven't you?'

It was not a remark he would have cared to make to any other officer of similar rank, and Moss spun round in amazement.

'Oh, I know about yourself and old Judge Raftery,' Tom said, keeping his fingers crossed that his career would not end with this pronouncement.

The Inspector's face remained hard and set, but his anger confined itself to the point at issue.

'So you know, do you? That venomous old toad took me from a good home and sentenced me to four years miserable existence, where I was neither cared for nor educated properly. Sometimes, it was a question of sheer survival; oh, I learned to defend myself in that place! And what was his reason, if you could dignify it by the name? Simply, that at seventeen Aunt Nellie was judged too young to have the care of her nine-year-old nephew. And if it hadn't been for Nellie getting married and she and her husband applying to the Court for custody, I'd have been shut away for three more years.'

He paused for breath, and Tom nodded sympathetically. 'So I heard,' Tom said, still in the same easy tone. 'A colleague of mine tipped me the wink, when he found out Finny and yourself were being put in harness together.'

There was silence between the two men and when next Moss spoke some of the violence had gone out of his voice. He left the window and came back to sit at the desk. 'That's in the past,' he said, 'better forgotten.' Then he added roughly: 'Finny himself was hardly born then, or only an infant.'

'Aye,' said the Sergeant, who prayed he was doing the right thing, 'that's what ye can't get out of your mind. Judge Raftery giving every care to his own son, while ye suffered the hardships!'

Another man would have abused him, but the blue eyes came up to meet his, and if the Sergeant did not like what he saw in their depths, he knew there was no attempt at concealment. There was hatred there, right enough.

Moss thumped the desk in an agonised

movement. 'Tom, it's been more than flesh and blood can stand; having him here day after day.'

At this, the door of the office opened, and the subject of the conversation entered, hesitatingly.

'Mr . . . er, Mr. Martin Lovell is here,' he said.

Before Moss could utter a word, Martin pushed into the room with the unconscious arrogance he sometimes displayed. 'Noonan tells me there's no word of Geraldine. Is that official? No word at all?'

Moss, who was speechless, shook his head.

'I see,' Martin Lovell said, 'well, some friends and I are going to try Blue Island. She may have gone there and got stuck with the mist. It's about the only place left for us to try.'

'Blue Island?' Moss repeated. 'It's a good thirty miles away.'

'Aye,' said the Sergeant, 'no place for a sailing boat. There's a deep channel, and rocks on either side.'

'Do you know it well, Sergeant?'

Martin enquired.

'Been there once or twice, sir.'

'I know it,' Moss said shortly.

His mind had switched back to grapple with the case. The mist was likely to remain for another seven to eight hours yet. All that the police could do here, was being done. If there was a chance, even a slim one . . .

He said: 'It's worth a try. If there's a police launch available in the area, we'll use that. Sergeant — get on the phone and see what you can do.'

Martin, delighted at this turn of events, said eagerly: 'We've already telephoned ahead, Inspector. There's a local boat standing by.'

'We may be forced to use it,' Moss conceded. 'However,' he turned to the Sergeant again, 'do the best you can, Tom. If anything should turn up here,' he added, 'contact the Windy Harbour station.'

'Right sir. Will you take Noonan with you? He has had plenty of experience, living on an island himself.'

'Can you spare him?'

'Haven't I about twenty other men here,' the Sergeant replied good-humouredly. 'Of course I can spare Noonan.'

Finny, who had no intention of being left out of the search party, thought it prudent to remain silent. From the baleful look Moss had given him, he had the feeling something pretty unpleasant was coming. Oh well, if only Geraldine were safe, he could stand the racket. The Sergeant, who read the young man's mind as if it had been laid bare before him, did his best to screen Finny from the Inspector's view until the little knot of persons at the door broke up and made for their cars outside, taking Finny with them.

As the Inspector came out to the door, the Sergeant put a hand on his shoulder. 'Take care of yourself, sir. Those rocks are no picnic.'

Moss seemed genuinely surprised at this display of concern and grunted something about 'being back in the morning.' He hurried out of the police station and got into his car. Noonan, who had gone back for his overcoat, hastened after him. The three cars drove away at speed.

Sergeant O'Shea felt it was incumbent on him to remain on duty all night, and in the morning he was rewarded with two phone calls, a visitor, and a letter from Mrs. Crotty, addressed to him personally, and which read as follows:

Dear Mr. O'Shea,

I write to tell you the good news that Lily has a son, a fine healthy boy, weighed eight pounds and has a head of hair. He is to be called Stanislaus, a name I never heard of and had to ask how to spell, but Lily says a boy without a father should have a name people will respect, and Stanislaus Sullivan is a fine name, I agree.

The other piece of news is that the lady in your post office whom Lily worked for and who was shot made a Will the day she died and left the shop to Lily, always provided she does not sell it for five years. Lily says she will come back to Gifford, although she never meant to. She says if Stanislaus has a bit of property at his back, what people say won't matter so much. I knitted him several little coats, but she says not to buy any more wool as I can have all I want from the shop.

Yours respectfully,
Ellen Crotty.

The Sergeant was so taken with this letter, he felt he must communicate its contents to Mrs. O'Shea. The rest of the morning's news was of a more dramatic nature.

17

Never did a town or village so deserve its name as did Windy Harbour. So Finny thought, as he observed it that night. Desolate, bleak, exposed; not a light showed in its small cottages or few great houses.

The men who travelled from Gifford reassembled on the quay at Windy Harbour and boarded a police launch which was waiting for them. As they packed into the launch, Finny hung back, waiting until almost all were aboard. Then he raised a large foot, trod firmly on the gangplank, and was unfortunate enough to meet his superior, in the teeth, as it were.

Much to his relief, Moss who was standing smoking his pipe in the stern, turned away at once and looked out to sea. Very little was visible. A mild south-west wind had developed and was gently wafting swirls of mist before it, but it was dark yet and would not be dawn for another two hours.

The powerful engine roared into life and then sank to a gentle purr as they slowly pulled out of the harbour and very cautiously made in the direction of the island.

Martin Lovell said: 'If this fails . . . '

Finny, who was behind him, put a hand on his shoulder. 'Don't think about that,' he said. 'We'll find her.'

Martin seemed grateful for this comfort. 'You're a good fellow, Finny,' was his rather gruff reply. 'Grace always said you were right for Geraldine. Sorry, I'm afraid I didn't see it myself at first.'

'I'm not sure Gerry sees it,' said Finny with a wry smile.

'Women never know what's good for them,' responded Martin, 'have to be told.'

'I'd say that would cause some fireworks.'

'Oh yes. She takes after Grace's old man. He was never one to tolerate interference.'

'So Dad said. He and your wife's father

were old friends.'

'Grace's father had no friends,' Martin replied, 'or if he had, he didn't deserve 'em. Treated them shamefully.'

'I think Dad understood him. He was a great man. His friends made allowances.'

'Your father knows about Gerry and yourself?'

'Yes.'

'How did he take it?'

'He didn't say anything against it. In fact, allowing for a small amount of legal caution, I believe he rather likes the idea.' Finny became silent and Martin, who it seemed, had been to Blue Island many times before, was swept into navigational discussions.

Noonan said: 'We'll have to find the channel. Too dangerous otherwise.'

'In that case we may have to wait until morning,' Moss replied.

Eventually, after taking a number of soundings and with many references to the charts which the local men had brought with them, they found the channel and Martin Lovell guided them into it. There was little wind, and they could feel the current underneath. Visibility was poor.

They began hailing from the launch. There was no reply.

'This side of the island is very exposed. Surely the *Emer* would have been spotted if she had anchored here before the fog.' This observation was made by Noonan, whose transposition to his native element had made him less in awe of his superiors.

Martin agreed, reluctantly: 'You'd think so; unless she was farther out to sea and only made it back here at the last moment.'

A shout from one of the men interrupted him, and all eyes strained in the direction of the man's pointing finger. The lights from the boat scarcely penetrated the surrounding murk, but the man seemed certain.

Then: 'I believe you're right,' Martin shouted. 'Pull over this way . . . gently now, easy . . . ' he gasped at the last moment, when they seemed to scrape past a rock only by a matter of inches. A jarring, thudding sound under their feet gave them a bad moment, and in the silence which followed, the Inspector made his first remark in quite a long while:

'If Miss Lovell brought the *Emer* in here, in fog, then she is a very remarkable yachtswoman indeed.'

'Did she know the channel?' Finny questioned, and her father, who was beside him assented. The older man's eyes were straining through the mist.

'Ahoy there,' he shouted. Then they all shouted together.

There seemed to be a very faint sound in reply.

At that moment, the launch gave a sickening lurch, and they found themselves apparently wedged between two rocks. The bottom appeared to be still free.

'Reverse the engine,' Martin said imperatively. 'Wait, hold it a second.'

The faint sound came closer, they all thought. 'Hold it there,' he said again.

The helmsman looked uneasy. 'A bit of a swell, sir, and we could get stove in, quick as a wink.'

The sound was heard again, and this time they knew it was a human voice.

'It's Gerry,' Finny cried, and he began to call to her, wildly and incoherently.

The amber fog lamps were turned in the direction of the faint sound, and this time Martin gave a shout:

'Gerry, it's me; Dad. We'll have you safe. Just hang on.' He made to clamber out of the launch, but the men around him held him back.

Moss Coen said: 'Better let one of our own men go. We'll reverse the boat and try to get in closer.'

'No, no,' Martin said hastily, 'we may miss her. One good shove, and I'll make it to the top of that rock. She's not so far above. I'm sure I can reach her.'

'Let me, sir,' Finny cut in. Before they could stop him, he had swung one long leg over the side and was poised to throw himself forward against the rock.

'Not that way!' Martin cried, seeing the danger of Finny being crushed, and then, as it was already too late to pull back: 'Hold the boat steady there,' he yelled.

Finny gave a sudden spring, his arms

outstretched, clawing for a precarious hold on the rock's jagged top, the sea's action having left the sides smooth and covered with slime. The men in the boat watched, unable to help, while he clambered about near the top unable to find a foothold. Then with one desperate effort, he heaved himself up, and his long bony hands grasped the top of the rock and he hauled himself to safety.

'Young fool never stopped to think how we're going to get him down again,' Moss growled.

Martin Lovell gripped the Inspector's arm suddenly, as scrambling sounds began to come from above the rock. He would have cried out, but Moss said: 'If it is your daughter, better not distract her.' Remembering Geraldine's climb up Gifford harbour wall, he added: 'She's not afraid of heights, anyway.'

Martin let that pass unquestioned. 'I should be up there,' he said in agony.

Finny, who had disappeared from their view, could be heard calling, and now they plainly heard a woman's voice answering. She seemed to be telling him to stay where he was.

'If only she doesn't fall . . . ' Martin whispered under his breath.

Then one of the men shouted: 'He's got her!'

The men in the boat listened, and after what seemed an age, two white faces peered out of the mist above them.

'Gerry,' her father called to her, 'are you all right?'

Her voice floated back, reassuring him.

'Right now,' interrupted the Inspector, resuming command, 'let's get busy. We'll try passing up a rope, if that's possible.'

One of the men behind him came forward with a good length of rope. Under Moss's instructions, he gave it a good swing out over the side. Finny made a grab for it, but it fell short. The man tried again, and this time the launch pushed in against the rock, driven by a rising swell.

'Look out!' the helmsman cried anxiously. He reversed the engine, and they edged back a small way.

'If we're going to do this, better get it done quickly,' Martin Lovell said anxiously.

This time Finny lay on top of the rock, Geraldine holding his legs. The rope swung, and he made a frantic effort to reach for it. Then, to the horror of the onlookers, his body seemed to arch suddenly and he overbalanced, desperately trying to get a handhold and failing, as the slippery rock face gave him no purchase.

Geraldine's cry: 'I can't hold on,' reached them just as they saw him slip from her grasp and plunge down the side of the rock and into the sea.

There was a second's stunned silence, then the men in the boat began calling.

Martin Lovell, already divesting himself of clothing, was stopped by the Inspector who took off his own coat and shoes. 'Still have to get your daughter back; you stay here for that job. Right,' Moss called to the others, 'two of you stay here; the other two come with me.'

The helmsman relinquished his post to Noonan, who like many islanders, was not a good swimmer, and he and another man took off their clothes and lowered themselves into the water.

Moss was already swimming strongly to the place where Finny had fallen in. He called back to the boat: 'Shine the lamp over here.'

The warm amber rays penetrated the swirling mist. 'Spread out,' Moss called to the other men, 'he may have drifted with the current.' There were sounds of energetic splashing.

Meanwhile, Martin's attention had again focused on his daughter. Unaided, she was now attempting to let herself down from the rock, holding on to the jagged part at the top and letting her long legs hang down on the smooth rock face beneath.

'Look out!' her father cried to his two companions, 'she's going to jump for it.'

Incredible as it seemed, this was his daughter's apparent intention; to scramble down and hope to land in the boat.

'She could injure herself bad,' said one of the men unnecessarily.

'We'll try to grab her,' cried Martin. 'Noonan, take the boat in as close as you can.'

Under Noonan's cautious navigation, the launch slowly edged forward. Martin and the other man spread out and linked arms. There was a grating sound of wood on stone.

'Jump now,' Martin yelled, and as she let go, they caught her neatly between them, staggering under her weight and all three landing in a heap on the deck.

'Oh Dad,' she said, as he hugged her to him, 'I never meant this to happen. The fog closed in before I could make it back. Have they got Finny yet?'

'Not yet,' he replied gently.

There was a call from one of the men in the water. 'We've lost the Inspector,' he shouted.

'Over here,' came a faint reply. 'Hurry . . . '

Those in the boat turned the lamp in the direction of the voice, and the men in the water swam towards the tiring Moss.

'He's got him!' Martin breathed, and Geraldine grasped her father's arm tightly. 'It'll be all right,' he reassured her. 'He has Finny. They're pulling him in now. It won't be long.'

But when they had helped to haul the missing Finny and his rescuers into the boat, Moss said urgently: 'We've got to work quickly; get any water out of his lungs.'

As two of the men did this, Martin, bending down, said to the Inspector: 'Better let me work on him. You're exhausted.'

Moss said: 'He has a bad gash on the temple.'

Martin made no reply but got to work grimly, one of the other men assisting.

Geraldine cried: 'Can't we get him to a hospital?'

For the first time, the Inspector seemed to notice her. 'Thank God you're off that rock,' he said. 'We're in no position to try winching at this stage.'

'Dad and another man helped me. Finny . . . is Finny going to be all right?'

'I don't know,' he said flatly. He was watching Martin's competent technique. The others had stripped off the wet clothes and wrapped the body in blankets.

Finny had been under the water when

Moss reached him. Rays from the fog lamp had penetrated the surface of the water, showing a patch of white in the depths beneath. When Moss dived, he had managed to grab hold of a limp arm.

Noonan now relinquished his post at the helm, and the launch headed back to Windy Harbour.

Martin Lovell continued working, sweat breaking out on his forehead. Geraldine sat beside the body, her face strained. She said: 'How long till we get him to a hospital?'

'Forget it,' was the Inspector's short reply. 'He'll be gone if we don't get him round before then. We tried to revive him while he was still in the water, but the current's so strong we could do very little.' Turning to Martin, Coen went on: 'Give him to me now; you have a rest.'

Geraldine got up, as Moss bent over the recumbent form.

'Dad,' she said brokenly, as her father reached out his arms to her, 'he's not going to die, is he?'

'Now, now,' Martin said soothingly, holding her to him, and stroking her hair, wet with mist, 'we have you safe.'

'I never thought it could end like this,' she cried. 'I thought everything would be all right now, but if Finny dies . . . ' She began to sob quietly.

The Inspector, for whom this artless speech had meaning, went on working. Exhausted, he eventually gave up his position to one of the other men.

'Is there any hope?' Martin asked.

Moss did not answer. The boat was speeding back at a reckless pace, the man at the wheel looking set and determined. Moss went over to him.

'It's no use,' he said. 'At this speed, we could have a head-on collision, and you won't save Raftery. When we get him ashore, it's still fifteen miles to the hospital.'

The speed slackened.

Noonan was tiring, and Moss said: 'Give him to me now.' He knelt down, and as Noonan drew back, Moss pounded at Finny's chest. Unbelievably, it seemed to them, there came a sound like a tiny hiccup.

'You've done it, I think!' Martin cried,

and the tears streamed down his daughter's face. Together the two men worked until the shallow breathing had strengthened, and the pulse could be felt, erratic though it might be. Presently, the eyelids fluttered open.

'Gerry,' the voice said faintly. She was on her knees beside him, stroking his hands. 'You're not hurt?' he breathed painfully.

'Not a scratch. Oh, Finny . . . '

He sighed and the eyelids closed again. She looked up alarmed, and reached across to her father.

'He'll be all right now,' Martin said. 'The Inspector has seen to that.'

Moss, who had been watching the pair of them, turned away, but Geraldine got to her feet and came over behind him, putting a hand on his arm. After an embarrassed pause, she said:

'I haven't been straight with you, about Simon I mean. It wasn't my secret and I couldn't tell anyone. But it doesn't matter now. When we get Finny to the hospital, you can hear the whole story; right from the beginning.'

Moss half smiled. 'We know who killed Simon Connolly,' he said. 'In fact, if it had not been for the false trails you've been blazing, we might have tumbled to it long ago.'

Geraldine looked at him wonderingly. 'You know who killed Simon; how long have you known?'

'Since I saw Clara Payne's wedding photograph,' Moss replied, fairly truthfully. He had the satisfaction of seeing his shot hit its mark.

18

When they finally returned to civilisation, Moss phoned the Sergeant.

'Any news of our man, Tom?'

'He's gone, sir, Left Dublin airport under his own name. Checked in at Heathrow twenty-five hours ago; stopping off, Panama. We haven't been able to trace further, as yet.'

'Under what name?'

'Kevin Flynn, sir.'

'Kevin Flynn!' Moss remembered his vigil at the Disco, and the subsequent report of the man they had had watching Geraldine Lovell.

'Anything from the real Mr. Flynn?'

'Yes. He reported his papers stolen.'

'When?'

'Yesterday evening.'

'When our man was safely gone, eh? We could make a case from the left-overs of this affair, Tom. However, that's up to the powers-that-be.'

'Did ye get Miss Lovell?'

'We did, and nearly drowned our poor Finny in the process. He'll pull through, though.'

The Sergeant exclaimed, and Moss said abruptly: 'Tell you when I see you, Tom.' He coughed. 'You may be interested to hear that Miss Lovell is now ready to make a full statement; now that it's too late of course. I've been very correct. Told her she could have her solicitor and all that. Martin Lovell is trying to shut her up, but the sight of Finny at death's door seems to have broken her resistance, and anyway I think she feels she owes me.'

'Why's that, sir?'

There was silence. Then Moss told him. His voice was not quite steady.

The Sergeant, with all the country-man's distaste of emotion (when sober) said rather desperately: 'That's splendid news, sir. His family will be very grateful to ye.'

'Coals of fire, eh?'

'When will ye be back, sir?'

'I'm afraid we're all-in. Finny's doing well in hospital. Miss Lovell and her father are at the hotel, and the rest of us have bunked down in the local police station. Later on, Martin is going out to the island again. The *Emer* is still anchored there and he wants to bring her in himself. I've made it clear to him that his daughter stays with us for the moment. I gather he's made her promise to keep quiet at least till they get back to Gifford . . . '

' . . . where his solicitor will be waiting,' interjected the Sergeant.

Moss laughed shortly. 'That's about it.'

The Sergeant had his own piece of news.

'Stanislaus Sullivan, eh? You've got to admire that girl.'

The Sergeant agreed that you had to, indeed. He wanted to ask Moss about a problem he had been chewing over since the day before, when Moss had discussed the case with him. However, the Inspector rang off abruptly, leaving O'Shea still undecided. As he said afterwards, having given the matter careful thought, he was actually on his way out of the station, when the subject of his deliberations met him at the gate.

'I should like a word with you, Sergeant,' Rachael Payne said.

'Come in, come in,' replied the Sergeant, metaphorically rubbing his hands.

But even he could not have expected the disclosures which followed.

Later that day, when he saw the document, Moss said: 'This makes a great deal of difference.'

'To the case against Geraldine Lovell, you mean?'

'Oh, I know she helped the fellow to escape; either stole the papers from Kevin Flynn, or else wormed them out of him — probably the latter. But it seems clear she never saw Connolly after he came back to this country. And Flynn, of course, has been very careful to say that he left his passport, visa etc. along with other papers, on the back seat of his car; stupid, if you like, but not necessarily criminal.'

'Will Miss Lovell be charged with helping in the escape?' enquired the Sergeant.

'If we can get our man back, it's possible.'

'What are the chances?'

'Of getting him back?' Moss shrugged his shoulders. 'What I can't get over,' he said, 'is Rachael Payne coming down to the station. Though, come to think of it, I suppose she was the obvious choice. Did she know what was in the statement?'

'It's difficult to say, sir.'

'Well, I shouldn't imagine he'd burden her with the contents, and also he'd be afraid she might tear it up, for the sake of the family. Still, she might have guessed something.'

'I shouldn't wonder,' the Sergeant replied.

That evening, a group of people assembled in the Lovells' elegant drawing-room. The Lovells, husband and wife, looked ill at ease and strained. In company with a wary Mr. Brennan, they sat together on the settee, and all three cast anxious eyes at the daughter of the house, who seemed so unconscious of her predicament as to be totally absorbed in the health and welfare of Mr. Finnbarr Raftery.

When not actually on the telephone

badgering the hospital authorities for up-to-date bulletins about their patient, Miss Lovell's sole topic was how wonderful the Inspector had been, and how grateful she was, sentiments which caused Mr. Brennan to say firmly: 'She's under great emotional stress, the poor girl.' And he glared at Moss.

The Inspector replied: 'Miss Lovell is not making a formal statement at this time; merely helping us to clear up a few relevant points in the case.'

The solicitor bristled. 'Which case is that?' he enquired.

'The case in which Owen Payne has admitted to the killing of his step-brother, Simon Connolly.'

Mr. Brennan shut his mouth with a snap, and his companions on the settee exclaimed in unison: 'Owen who?'

Geraldine, who had thrown a grateful glance at Moss, said at once: 'Owen Connolly; he wasn't legally a Connolly. He is Peter Connolly's son. Clara Payne is his mother.'

'Well!' exclaimed Grace, looking at her daughter in astonishment. 'I've lived here

307

all my life, and I've never heard anything of this.'

'Nevertheless, we believe it to be true,' Moss said firmly. Turning to Geraldine, he went on: 'Owen told you?'

She nodded. 'His mother was fifteen, when it happened. Peter was a year or two older. They wanted to get married, only the Paynes wouldn't have Peter Connolly, baby or no baby. That was why Owen was so upset about Lily; it was like history repeating itself.'

'Did he know Simon meant to ditch Lily?'

'Yes. He found out when Simon came back here.'

'What was the motive?'

'He never meant to kill Simon. They had a row and he went for him, and knocked him down. He didn't even know Simon was dead, at first. He just went off and left him lying there. He was all worked up about Lily, and Simon taking Rachel's brooch, and about me too.'

Mr. Flannan Brennan here gave a warning cough, but Moss went on as though there had been no interruption.

'Owen was upset about Simon breaking with you; Simon did break the engagement — it wasn't that you found out about Lily being pregnant?'

'I really do think,' began Mr. Brennan, when Geraldine turned to him.

'Oh, do shut up, please. We'll never get finished if you keep interrupting.'

Grace Lovell said: 'Geraldine!'

In spite of his anxiety, Martin couldn't help grinning. Sitting quite relaxed in the armchair, seldom had his daughter more nearly resembled her grandfather.

'You asked me about Simon and me . . . ' Geraldine turned again to Moss. 'Simon found out about a brooch Rachel Payne had; it was a family heirloom . . . oh, you know about that, do you? Well, anyhow, he stole it and then began looking for a way to get it out of the country. He hit on the idea of using Lily as cover. He knew if he suddenly went away on his own, it might look suspicious. Of course he never stopped to think ahead, but that was Simon all over.

'Anyway, I was bitter at the way he just came in one day and said it was all off between us, and demanded his ring back. It took me a week or so to figure out I was mad to think of marrying him anyway, and unfortunately in the meantime I met Owen and poured out my wrongs. I knew he was always rather keen on me; I mean the way he told me about his mother and that. He never told anyone else. For instance, Margaret Connolly didn't know; still doesn't, I imagine.'

'Well!' Geraldine went on, taking a deep breath, and extricating herself from a tangle of information, 'that was why, afterwards, I felt partly responsible.'

'A mere schoolgirl scruple,' Mr. Brennan interjected.

Geraldine regarded him frankly. 'I expect it might seem that way to you, you're so used to criminal cases. But if Owen hadn't been so mad at his brother, Simon would still be alive.'

Mr. Brennan, who had never appeared in a criminal court in his life, looked seriously put out. Before he could reply, however, Geraldine was speaking again:

'After the body was discovered, and I

heard about the blanket, and Simon being nicely laid out, and above all about the Payne family grave, somehow, well, it just had to be Owen. I was frantic to know, and I went straight round and asked him. He told me the truth. I think he was glad to be able to tell someone. He explained about the brass plate. He was sure the police would find it. He said: 'If they trace that, I'm done for.' Indeed, I told him I'd . . .'

Here, Mr. Brennan gestured in some alarm, and Moss who could well believe the enterprising Miss Lovell had suggested a little late night digging, gave a grim smile. No doubt the more prudent Owen had firmly vetoed the idea.

Geraldine gave Moss a speaking look. 'Where was I?' she asked.

'Owen had left Simon up at the ruin, and according to him, didn't know his brother was dead. When did he find out?'

'He came back later that night. He got sorry, and he wanted to be sure Simon was all right. That was typical of Owen. Anyhow, there was Simon stone cold. Owen stayed there most of the night.

Then he put the body into his car and drove down to his own farm. Afterwards, when he had everything ready, he came back one night, and let himself into the cemetery. Kevin Bates wouldn't admit it, of course, but it's only since this thing happened that he makes sure to lock the gate every night.'

'What about the brooch?'

Grace Lovell felt she had been silent long enough. 'Geraldine, my dear,' she interrupted, 'won't you let Mr. Brennan advise you. That's what he's here for, to help you.'

The solicitor smiled thinly and nodded his approval. Addressing himself to Geraldine, he went on: 'Now, if I might be allowed to suggest . . . '

Geraldine turned on him swiftly: 'For the last time,' she said furiously, 'if you won't be quiet, I shall go down to the police station with Inspector Coen, where we can talk in peace.'

With a glare, Mr. Brennan subsided, but Martin got to his feet, and came and sat on the arm of his daughter's chair. He looked down at her. 'I should be opposed to any such move,' he said.

Geraldine regarded him affectionately. 'Dad,' she said, putting her hand on his arm. 'Now, oh yes, about the brooch. That was how Simon came back to this country. When Owen found out Rachel Payne's brooch had been stolen; I don't know why, but he immediately suspected Simon. Perhaps Rachel told him something to give him that idea. Anyhow, he tried to get the brooch back. He wrote offering Simon money — not the value of it, he didn't have that much — and that's what brought Simon home.

'Owen found the brooch on Simon's body that night, and afterwards he decided to try to put it back without anyone knowing. With Rachel out of the house, he got in and hunted around to leave it where, when she found it, she might believe it had been merely mislaid.'

'And in so doing, he found the blanket?'

'Yes, Simon had been dead for three days, and he was still trying desperately to figure out what to do about the body . . . '

'Why didn't he simply come forward

and admit to what had happened? If it's true he never meant to kill his brother, the charge would most likely be manslaughter. And taking into account some of Simon's activities, a jury might well take a lenient view.'

'Oh, don't you see,' she cried, 'that was partly the reason. Simon's taking the brooch would have had to come out, and all about Lily, and Owen's real name. His stepfather doesn't even know about Owen.'

'Still,' Moss said gently, 'Clara must be nearly fifty. Wouldn't she face a scandal rather than see her son adrift on the other side of the world, homeless, without a future?'

She lifted her head, and he saw there were traces of tears in her eyes.

'It was his decision,' she said.

After all that had happened, it was an irony Moss felt, that he who had envied Finnbarr Raftery for so long, envied him now more than ever.